The Cowboy Inherits a Bride

By Cora Seton

Author's Note

The Cowboy Inherits a Bride is a prequel to the **Cowboys of Chance Creek** series but can easily be read as a standalone novella at any time. To find out more about Ethan, Cab, Rob and Jamie and the other inhabitants of Chance Creek, Montana, be sure to read the other novels in the series, including:

The Cowboy's E-mail Order Bride (Volume 1)
The Cowboy Wins a Bride (Volume 2)
The Cowboy Imports a Bride (Volume 3)
The Cowgirl Ropes a Billionaire (Volume 4)
The Sheriff Catches a Bride (Volume 5)
The Cowboy Lassos a Bride (Volume 6)
The Cowboy Rescues a Bride (Volume 7)
The Cowboy Earns a Bride (Volume 8)

Look for the **Heroes of Chance Creek** series, too:

The Navy SEAL's E-mail Order Bride (Volume 1)
The Soldier's E-Mail Order Bride (Volume 2)
The Marine's E-Mail Order Bride (Volume 3)
The Navy SEAL's Christmas Bride (Volume 4)
The Airman's E-Mail Order Bride (Volume 5)

Sign up for my newsletter HERE.
www.coraseton.com/sign-up-for-my-newsletter

Chapter One

SUNSHINE PATTERSON STRODE down a cracked and
pitted sidewalk on the wrong side of a very small
town. In fact, she wasn't sure Chance Creek, Montana,
even deserved that designation. It was the kind of place
you passed on the freeway from one city to the next—a
grid of streets surrounded by miles and miles of pastures, rivers and far off mountains. If she was honest, its
rural location made her downright nervous, but there
was no turning back now.

Her beaded kitten heels rubbed a blister on her little
toe, her shoulder ached from lugging her overstuffed
jute handbag, and her wheeled suitcase bumped and
jerked over every crack in the cement as she dragged it
behind her. The bus ride from Chicago had been a
nightmare of men with body odor, screaming small
children and pimply faced teenagers dressed all in black,
and the cabbie who brought her most of the way from
the bus station had dropped her off unceremoniously
four blocks from her destination when she informed
him that smoking in a taxi was against the law.

But those were minor irritants compared to the

events of the last month. She had already brushed them off.

This was the first day of her new life—a life without Greg Albright—and nothing could stop her from showing him she didn't need him or his award-winning organic restaurant. No longer was she the kind of naïve young woman who invested all her savings into her boyfriend's bistro, only to find out he was sleeping with one of the waitresses. From now on she was the kind of woman who went her own way and owned her own business, thank you very much.

Thank God Aunt Cecily had left her a property in downtown Chance Creek as an inheritance or she would be sleeping on the streets of Chicago right now. Her parents would always take her in, of course, but there was no way she was returning to Lake Forest to face a chorus of *I told you so's* from them.

Chance Creek was a steep step down from Chicago, but she refused to dwell on that. She wouldn't be here long, anyway. She had a plan. She would start with a small vegan cafe in the building Cecily had left her. Within the year, she would sell the business and graduate to a larger restaurant—perhaps in Billings. Five years from now, when she had taken Montana by storm with her cutting-edge vegan creations, she would make the leap back to Chicago and show Greg just what a phony wanna-be he was compared to her own brilliance as a chef and restaurateur.

Not that she was looking for payback. Bad karma and all that. Sunshine sighed and picked up her pace.

What she really wanted was smoking hot sex with a man who could make her forget Greg ever existed. Unfortunately, she doubted she'd find such a man within a hundred miles of sleepy little Chance Creek.

She navigated her way around a particularly nasty crack in the sidewalk. Four blocks ago, when she'd exited the cab, she'd been pleased to find herself in a well-kept-up neighborhood of small homes and shops. She'd even passed a bookstore and a cute little diner she immediately took note of as a potential rival for her customers. After two blocks of walking, the shops were gone but the neighborhood seemed solid enough. Two more brought a distinct drop in quality of both the curb appeal of the homes and their inhabitants. Sunshine had pointedly ignored the stares and comments from a group of men loitering around a truck up on blocks in front of one of the more run-down houses. The few shops here showed a serious level of decay. She bit her lip and noted how a little elbow grease and some money... well, a lot of money... could really spiff things up. The wheels of her suitcase got stuck in another crack and she stopped and fished her cell phone out of her bag. Balancing the slim phone on one shoulder against her cheek, she took hold of her things and teetered onward. "Hi Kate, it's me," she said when her friend picked up. "I'm almost there. Just another block."

"Why are you panting?" Kate's cultured voice made Sunshine long for her company. She could use a friend by her side right now.

"I asked the cabbie to stop smoking and he, in turn,

asked me to get out of his car a few blocks early."

Kate chuckled. "When are you going to learn to let sleeping dogs lie?"

Sunshine could picture her friend at her desk at the law firm of Simons and Schiller back in Chicago, where she'd already worked her way into a junior partnership. Kate was always cool and collected, always knew exactly what she wanted and got it. Her fiancé, if she ever decided she wanted one, wouldn't steal her money and kick her to the curb. And despite what she'd just said, when Kate told cab drivers to put out their cigarettes, they did.

"Probably not in this lifetime."

There was a pause, in which Kate evidently decided her point had been sufficiently made. "So—what's the neighborhood like? Overrun with cowboys?"

"Not exactly. It's got lots of potential, though. Lots of character." She tried to believe her own words. If one more thing went wrong she might sit down on the sidewalk and cry.

"Right." There came the clicking of fingernails on a keyboard. Kate was multi-tasking, as usual. "Can you see your café yet?"

That brought a smile to Sunshine's face. *Her* café. She liked the sound of that. This time she wouldn't have a partner. She planned to do everything herself. She couldn't get screwed if no one was there to do the screwing.

"Not yet. Any minute." She crossed a street and found herself on a block that seemed almost abandoned. Several older automobiles sat parked at the curb. A barbershop edged the opposite corner, next to a pawn shop and a corner store. All three storefronts sported iron bars over their windows. On her side of the street, she confronted an empty lot sprouting weeds and cast-off tires. It grew a healthy crop of broken glass and liquor bottles, too. She tottered past it uncertainly.

"Well?" Kate asked. "I'm breathless from the suspense. What does it look like?" From the tapping sounds carrying across the phone line, Sunshine deduced her friend wasn't too breathless to work.

Sunshine approached the building whose street address matched the one on the letter she'd received from Aunt Cecily's solicitor. It was large, square, and sided with blue metal. A wide shop window framed what looked to be an expansive waiting room of some sort. Sunshine shaded her eyes to see inside better. A shoddy wooden counter separated the seating area—done in cracked brown tile and plastic chairs—from whatever went on in the rest of the building. A gap to the right of the counter led to a door to the back.

"Well?"

"It's..." Sunshine's gaze slid upward to take in the large painted sign over the entrance to this monstrosity. "It's... a rifle range."

"What?" The incessant clicking of her friend's fingers on the keyboard stopped and Sunshine knew she had Kate's full attention now. "Your aunt left you a rifle range?"

"That's what the sign says. An indoor rifle range. Is

that even possible?"

"Send me a picture. Now."

Sunshine did as she was told and snapped a picture that would show Kate everything. No sense trying to hide this latest disaster. Not from her best friend. When she got back on the line, Kate whistled.

"I think I've heard of indoor rifle ranges, but there must be some mistake. I thought your aunt left you a restaurant."

"She did. I think. There's some sort of space up front, and…" Sunshine craned her neck and made out the unmistakable shape of a refrigerator behind the counter, along with a stove. A sinking feeling in her stomach told her that maybe she was the one who had made the mistake. Had Aunt Cecily left her part of a building? Or a building already rented to someone else? Would she be able to evict the tenant anytime soon? Where was the apartment Cecily had promised her?

"Is the rifle range occupied? Can you hear shots?" Kate's voice brought her back to the present.

"No… wait." Now that she was paying attention, she heard muffled thumps that could be shots fired inside the building. Her blood pressure ratcheted up another notch. "Yes—someone's shooting in there. In my building! What do I do?" Her voice squeaked on her last sentence and she willed herself to calm down.

"Is the solicitor there?"

Trust Kate to be practical. "No. Wait… maybe." A man in a suit stood up from one of the plastic chairs in the waiting room and made his way to the door. He pushed it open and stuck his head out. "Miss Patterson?"

"Yes," she called and then spoke into the phone. "He's here. I've got to go."

"Call me the minute you find out what's going on."

"I will." Her throat was dry and her hands slippery with perspiration as she slipped her phone into her purse and waited for the man in the suit. She noticed through the dirty plate glass window that the other occupants of the waiting room were taking a distinct interest in this meeting. All in their late twenties or early thirties, except for an older gentleman who could have been one of their fathers, to a man they wore jeans, work shirts, and cowboy hats. She couldn't see their feet, but she'd bet they'd all have boots on. At least they weren't as bad as the men down the block. She didn't peg them as troublemakers—just not the kind of men who favored vegetarian restaurants. One of them turned toward the back of the building and gave a shout. Was he calling the rifle range's owner?

She turned her attention to the man who had come outside to meet her. He was balding, in his fifties, she estimated, exuding an air of distraction which didn't inspire confidence. How she wished for someone like Kate beside her. Someone who would cut through all the baloney and lay things on the line.

"Miss Patterson, I'm Abe Moffat. We spoke on the phone."

"Hi, Abe. Call me Sunshine, please."

"Sunshine. Lovely name." He seemed at a loss for

what to say next. They surveyed the building in front of them uncertainly. "So. Here it is."

"Yes. I… uh… didn't realize there was a tenant in it."

"Well, yes. I believe I mentioned that there was an irregularity in your inheritance, Miss… Sunshine."

"No, I don't think you did, actually." She tried to channel Kate. Kate wouldn't put up with any of this.

"Well, it is a little peculiar." Abe reached into a pocket, brought out a cloth handkerchief, and mopped his face with it. Sunshine wasn't sure she'd ever seen anyone actually use a cloth handkerchief. "I decided to check into it a bit with one of my colleagues from Billings before bringing it to your attention. Maybe we should go somewhere else to talk," he said, glancing at the audience in the rifle range's waiting room.

She followed his gaze and nearly stopped breathing as a man walked out of the back to stand at the counter. He was tall, broad-shouldered and suntanned, with hawk-like features and a stare that pinned her in place from thirty feet away. As much as she wanted to escape his eagle-eyed gaze, she had an equal and opposite urge to preen under it. Now that was a man, and Greg… Greg could have his sordid waitress fling, because Greg wasn't fit to tie this guy's shoelaces.

"No, Mr. Moffat. I'd like to stay right here while you explain what the irregularity with my inheritance is." She found it hard not to stare right back at the man at the inside counter. How tall was he? Six foot one? What would it feel like to rest her cheek on one of those broad shoulders?

Abe swallowed hard. "All right. I'll try to explain. Your aunt found herself in a bit of a predicament when she wrote her will. Perhaps you should read her own words on the subject."

Sunshine tore her gaze away from the window and waited for the lawyer to fish a faded envelope from the folder in his hands and give it to her. Drawing out a sheet of paper filled with Aunt Cecilia's looping scrawl, she held it up and squinted to make out her aunt's words. The letter was dated some three months ago, two months before Aunt Cecily passed away.

Dear Sunshine,

I'm afraid I've done it again. I know I promised you a restaurant when you graduated from the culinary institute, but then you and Greg joined forces and were doing so well for yourselves with Chez Rosetta, that when a friend hit a rough patch I thought you'd never miss the old thing. However, from what you've let slip during your recent visit, I predict tough times ahead for you, honey. And now I'm in a real pickle. I've promised my building twice over, to two young people I really care for. All I can do is give you both a fair shake at it. After all, it is large and should contain enough room for each of you to pursue your dreams.

Abe will explain everything and I know it will all turn out for the best. It always does, doesn't it?

Love,
Aunt Cecily

Her aunt's words splashed over her like a bucket of ice water. "I have to share the building?"

"It's kind of a contest."

She blinked. "A contest? What does that mean?" She had banked everything on having a place to live and a café to run. This couldn't be happening.

The lawyer was clearly uncomfortable. "Cecily has stipulated that each of you must occupy the building continually for four months. You must run a business— a restaurant in your case, the rifle range in his—and live on the premises. If you abandon the premises, and she defines abandonment as spending more than one single night away from the building, Cole Linden immediately has the right to purchase it outright from you for a sum set by Cecily."

Sunshine couldn't believe her ears. This was ludicrous. "How much?"

"How much...?" he echoed.

"What's the *sum set by Cecily*?" Maybe it would be enough for her to start over somewhere else. Somewhere more appropriate.

Abe licked his lips. "Sixty."

"Sixty thousand dollars?" That was outrageous for a building this large—it must be worth five times as much.

"Sixty dollars, actually."

Sunshine's mouth dropped open. Sixty dollars wouldn't cover a bus ticket back to Chicago. Why would Aunt Cecily do this to her? She glanced through the plate glass window at the man who leaned against the counter, his hands braced against it as he took her measure. "Is that Cole Linden?"

Abe nodded.

She met the man's gaze, pressing her lips together in a thin line. Who cared how hot he was? The bastard had weaseled his way into Cecily's good graces and stolen her inheritance out from under her.

"Is this his business? His... rifle range?"

"Yes." Abe took a step back, as if afraid she might lash out. Well, he should be afraid. They all should. This was her building. Her restaurant. And that man—Cole—was using it to promote violence and murder. Those cowboys in the waiting room were nothing more than thugs.

Cole Linden stared right back at her. He probably sensed she was a card-carrying member of PETA from where he stood. "What if he spends more than one night away?" She could arrange for that—just break both his legs and dump him near the Canadian border. Unless he shot her first.

"Then you immediately inherit the building free and clear. But..." He held up a finger. "In either case, the absence may not be caused by the person who stands to inherit from it."

Damn.

"What happens at the end of four months?"

"If neither of you abandon the building, then it comes down to earnings. The person with the more successful business wins."

Well. At least that was something. Crazy Aunt Cecily

must have known she'd take the challenge and succeed without a problem. Cole Linden and his stupid rifle range would be out of here in no time.

"Fine. But where exactly am I supposed to run my restaurant?"

"There." Abe gestured to the waiting room and counter. Sunshine squinted against the glare on the plate glass window. The stove behind the counter did have six burners. She thought she saw a sink, as well. The waiting room, while large, was no restaurant, however. She stifled an urge to shake the man. She'd have to bust her ass to transform the place into anything a respectable person would want to visit. "Where's my apartment?"

Abe seemed to have something caught in his throat. "There's an entrance at the side of the building. It's... cozy. And... it's not exactly *your* apartment." The lawyer's face went somewhat pink. His paisley tie seemed about to choke him.

She shut her eyes and counted to ten. "Spill it."

Abe shuffled the papers he clutched in his hands. "You'll have to share it with Mr. Linden."

"COLE, COME HERE—you've got to see this!"

Cole Linden carefully locked up the ammunition cabinet, exited the storeroom his father had converted to a safe room, and made his way to the front of the building where five men watched Abe Moffat confront a young woman who was decidedly angry. Cole didn't recognize the woman. The men in the waiting room he'd known all his life.

Ethan Cruz headed up one of the oldest ranches around now that his father had just passed away. He was engaged to the pretty but petulant Lacey Taylor, a girl Cole had known since she wore her hair in pigtails. Jamie Lassiter was a hired hand on Ethan's ranch, and his best friend. He had a way with horses that would keep him in demand no matter where he went, but he was loyal to Ethan. Cab Johnson, a large but quiet man, was the local sheriff. He'd ended up with the post when his father could no longer do the job. Cab was young to be an elected official, but he was well respected around town. Rob Matheson was a jokester, but a hard worker. One of four sons, he lived on the Double-Bar-K, the spread next to the Cruz ranch, which his father, Holt Matheson—currently occupying the seat beside him—ruled with an iron fist.

Cole had known every one of them for most of his life and appreciated their patronage—especially when they could have ridden out on their own spreads and tested any weapon they wanted without bothering anyone.

The only man to enter the range today that he didn't know well was the lawyer who'd brought him the news a week ago of Cecily Silverton's arrangement. News that left him shell-shocked in a way he hadn't thought possible. Sure, he'd known there was a chance that Cecily's death meant an end to the sweet deal that allowed him to keep the rifle range his father had opened twenty years ago, but she had always hinted she meant to leave the building to him, and she hadn't seemed like the type to lie to a man.

But Cecily hadn't left the building to him, at least not outright. She'd left it jointly to him and some silver-spoon niece of hers who probably spent all her time shopping and talking on the phone. He still had a chance to get the building—for the bizarre price of sixty dollars—if the interloper bailed within four months. But if she didn't, said niece would be his new landlord. If she allowed him to stay. Meanwhile, he had to share not only the building with whatever cockamamie business the debutante came up with, he'd have to share his apartment, too. His one bedroom, one bath, eight-hundred-square-foot apartment.

And what about the rest of his business? He'd still been in the Army, fighting in Iraq, when his father sent him the paperwork that made him a joint owner of Linden Holdings. It had never occurred to him not to sign, but now he knew that instead of a thriving busi-ness, he'd become partners in an enterprise drowning in debt. At the time, Linden Holdings had consisted of this building, two apartment buildings and the accoutre-ments of his father's deep-sea diving operation. Diving for treasure was Bailey Linden's passion. Thousands of miles away in a foreign desert, Cole hadn't realized his father had mortgaged everything else to the hilt to fund his trips until a new batch of paperwork had arrived in the mail for him to sign—paperwork that spelled out the deal his dad had struck with Cecily.

His father had told him they had no choice but to

sell the range building to her, but had assured him it was only a temporary setback. Cole cursed himself for not asking the tough questions. He'd been too young to push his father for answers back then, and too ignorant to even know what to ask.

Now he knew all too well. His father had passed away less than a year after Cole left the Army and came home. When he took over the day-to-day operations, the amount of debt Linden Holdings was carrying staggered him. His accountant had sat him down and outlined the process of bankruptcy, but Cole refused to go that route. That would mean certain eviction for the tenants in his apartments—some of whom he'd known since he was a child.

But without the range, how was he supposed to keep paying down the mortgage on the two apartment buildings that stood on the back end of the property it fronted? Heaven knew the buildings should be paying their own way, but they weren't. Not with all the renovations they'd required in the last five years. He'd had to replace the roofs, rebuild the stairs, buy a brand-new hot water tank along with new appliances for most of the units. And don't even get him started on all the new flooring he'd put in to replace the decades-old carpets.

What the hell was Cecily thinking? He'd always liked the old woman, had been genuinely sorry when she passed away. Cecily was sweet to purchase the broken-down building and allow them to pay token rent to keep the range running. From time to time she'd stopped by, drunk a cup of the coffee he kept brewing all day for his customers, and seemed to take genuine pleasure in watching the men fire their various firearms at the paper targets in the shooting lanes. Cecily was great. But this... Sunshine... would be something altogether different. He was doomed and so was his range—and all the people who lived in his apartments, too.

He shoved aside a pile of paperwork as he watched the blonde question Abe. Maybe he deserved to lose it all. A better businessman than him would have raised the rents to twice as much as they were now, but over the years his father had accumulated Chance Creek's misfits and downtrodden. Cole couldn't bear to kick out any of them, or to watch their faces when he delivered the news that their apartments would no longer be affordable. He knew most of them were keeping afloat by the skin of their teeth, just like he was. Liliana Warner was a single mother who worked as a housekeeper at the Big Sky Hotel. William Lake was eighty-two and living on a fixed income. Scott Preston, a veteran who'd fought in Iraq, was supporting two sets of grandparents on his disability payments. How could he turn any of them out, let alone the others?

The worst part was he didn't have a dime saved to start over somewhere new even if he walked away from the company's debts. After five years of living on ramen noodles, Cole could see his way clear to putting his balance sheets back into the black soon, but if he lost the range, he'd lose the apartments, too, and then he'd have nothing. No business, no savings. He'd be starting over at twenty-nine. Some developer would come in and buy the apartments for pennies on the dollar, kick out the current tenants, do a nominal renovation, jack the prices up as high as the market would bear and make a killing.

He hated to think ill of Cecily, not after all she'd done for his family over the years, but if she wasn't going to leave the building to him, he wished she'd never even hinted at it. Losing it felt too much like a well-aimed kick to his nuts.

He took a deep breath as he focused on the woman outside the building. Holy cow, she was a knock-out. He leaned against the counter for a better look.

Holt cackled in his corner. "Thought you'd be interested."

"That's your new roommate? Lucky break." Jamie was staring at her too.

"Not bad," Ethan agreed.

"Wouldn't mind seeing that at the breakfast table," Rob threw in for good measure.

Cab held his peace and so did Cole. Pretty is as pretty does. She was definitely good looking, curved in all the right places with long, free-flowing shiny blonde hair that made her name not quite as ridiculous as it would otherwise be. She wore black leggings, and a nut-brown tunic that showed her curves to perfection. Her shoes were silly—tiny heeled things with thin beaded straps to hold them precariously on her feet. She had the determinedly healthy look he associated with yoga instructors. How old could she be—twenty-four, twenty-five, maybe?

This was his new landlord?

And roommate.

Lucky him.

"I'll bet that lawyer's explaining the details of Cecily's will," Holt said, and proceeded with a running commentary which nicely complemented the range of expressions flitting across the young woman's face. Shock, surprise, anger, horror—it would have been humorous if he hadn't known exactly how she felt. Then she looked in the window, met his gaze, and Cole felt like he'd been shot through the heart. She was more than pretty; she was drop-dead beautiful, with wide, expressive eyes and full lips that promised she could get up to all kinds of passionate shenanigans with the right partner.

He was not the right partner.

Although he would be a partner of sorts if she took her aunt's challenge and moved in with him for four months.

He straightened up and cleared his throat when he noticed the grins on his audience's faces. "She might bail. A girl like that isn't going to want to move into a rifle range, right?"

"Looks like a spitfire to me," Holt said.

"Cole can handle her," Jamie said. "He'll make her life so miserable she'll turn tail and run within the week. Within the day, even. Right, Cole?"

That's certainly the way he'd intended to play it, but now he wasn't so sure. Cecily wasn't a stupid woman and she didn't have a speck of malice in her. She wasn't one to lead a guy on for several years and then pull the rug out from under his feet. What if he was reading the situation all wrong? What if she'd had a plan of her own when she set up her will this way?

He watched the slender blonde gesticulate angrily at the lawyer outside. Abe looked pained and he had no doubt the man wished he hadn't been given this particular job to carry out. Even angry, Sunshine was beautiful. She looked smart, passionate, perhaps kindhearted.

Cole's next thought made his fingers press harder into the counter. Had Cecily left him *Sunshine* in her will?

And did he want to accept this bequest?

A smile curved his mouth as he considered this possibility. One look at Sunshine squaring her shoulders and approaching the front door told him she'd girded her loins for a knock-down, drag-out battle of the sexes, but suddenly he was sure he could win the prize without throwing even one punch.

Ethan glanced up and met his gaze. The rancher chuckled. "I've seen that look before. You've got a plan, don't you?"

"Yep."

They all jumped when the door banged open and the woman in question strode across the tile floor. "Cole Linden?" she said, stopping on the opposite side of the counter. She ignored Jamie's frank perusal and the muffled laughter coming from the rest of the crew.

"That's me." He forced himself to meet her gaze

without blinking, found himself holding his breath to find out what she was going to do next.

"My name's Sunshine Patterson and I'm moving in. You have an hour to clear your things out of my apartment."

He raised an eyebrow. "You mean *my* apartment, don't you?"

Her jaw tightened. "*Our* apartment, Mr. Linden. I'll need the bedroom and half of the space in all the other rooms. I suggest you get to it right away."

Cole rocked back on his heels, surprised at how much it pleased him she was going through with this. After all, she could turn out to be a real pain in the ass.

Somehow he didn't think so. Somehow he thought she was going to be the most fun he'd had in a long time.

"There's only one bedroom and I'm already using it. I suggest you find some nice swanky hotel for the night."

That seemed to catch her off balance. She glanced away, squared her shoulders again and looked him right in the eye. "You wish. You and I both know I'm not spending a single night of the next hundred and twenty away from that apartment. This is my building and come fall I'll be waving bye-bye to you as you drive away with all your stupid guns."

"Firearms," five voices automatically corrected her. Cole squashed the smile that threatened to quirk his lips. Miss Sunshine had a lot to learn, and he'd be happy to teach her.

Jesus, he needed to get his mind out of his pants. At least for the moment. Plenty of time to go down that road later. Four whole months to be exact.

"I'm a woman. I need my own bedroom," Sunshine said. "You can take the couch."

Cole knew everyone was waiting to hear his next words. Knew also that if he blinked, he might as well walk away from the rifle range right now.

"Make me."

She flushed, and her eyes sparked with rage and something else. Tears? Heaven help him. Before he could react to them, though, she'd blinked them away and whirled around to stretch a hand out to Abe the lawyer.

"Give me the keys. If Mr. Linden can't be bothered to move his things, I'll have to do it for him."

She snatched the key the lawyer produced from his pocket and was out the door before any of them could move. She shooed away the transient man who had sidled out from an alley to check out the luggage she'd left on the street and began to haul it over to the side of the building where the entryway to the apartment was located.

"You gonna go after her?" Ethan asked.

"I guess so."

Right after he caught his breath.

Chapter Two

S UNSHINE'S PHONE RANG again when she reached the brown steel door that led to her new home. Her hands were shaking when she fished it out of her purse, put it to her ear and simultaneously fit the key Abe had given her into the lock. She couldn't believe she had to spend the next four months living in this dump with a complete stranger—a stranger whose presence unnerved her in ways she didn't care to examine too deeply. His hands splayed on the chipped countertop of the rifle range were so large and capable—not at all like Greg's manicured hands. His shoulders were broad enough to hold up a world of troubles, and his face—his face took her breath away.

"Hello?" The key slid home and she turned the handle.

"It's me. What's happening?" Kate said.

"You won't believe it. I don't believe it and I'm here."

"That good?"

"That bad. Not only is the place a rifle range and a dump, the inheritance is encumbered."

"How?" Kate assumed her lawyer tone.

"In order for me to keep the building, I have to occupy it for four months, at which point I own it free and clear."

"Okay. You planned on doing that anyway. Is that all?"

"No." Sunshine tried to push open the door, but it didn't budge. She angled her body sideways to it and gave it a good shove with her right hip. "I not only have to run my café here, I have to live here. Kate, I have to share an apartment with the owner of the rifle range for the next four months. A one bedroom apartment. If I spend more than one night away, I lose the whole thing!" Her voice wavered.

The silence on the other end was ominous. "Kate? Are you still there?" Sunshine stood outside her new home, her shoulders slumped and her optimistic attitude lying in tatters at her feet. "Kate?"

"Send me a copy of the will," Kate said with a sigh. "I'll see what I can do. Meanwhile, don't budge. Follow Cecily's instructions to the letter."

"But—"

"To the letter." Kate hung up with a click. Sunshine looked at the phone, then took a deep breath. She'd send the copy of the will right away. If anyone could fix this, Kate could.

With renewed determination, she gave the door one more good shove and it swung inwards with a painful groan. Sunshine gathered her luggage and awkwardly crossed the threshold into a small foyer. She noted with surprise that it was neat, with a decent side table on which lay several pieces of mail and a copper bowl she guessed held Cole's keys when he was at home. She could take in almost the entire apartment from where she stood. The foyer opened out into a large living space. To her left lay an eating area and a kitchen separated from it by a low counter. Straight ahead and to her right was the living room area. One door led to a small bathroom. Another to the single bedroom.

The place was full of masculine, oversized furniture. A flat-screen television took pride of place in one corner, with a sofa positioned for the best viewing. Several bookshelves were filled with books, a point in Cole's favor in her eyes. The kitchen was tiny—just a stove, refrigerator and sink, with minimal cabinets and counter space. There was no dishwasher, she saw with a groan. A serviceable dinner table with four chairs made up the dining area.

The only thing that seemed out of place in this masculine haven was a large artistic photograph hanging on the wall behind the table. It showed a meadow full of wildflowers in bloom in the midst of a cityscape, with apartment buildings on either side and a dilapidated warehouse in the background. It was certainly striking, but she would have expected something more along the lines of an Ansel Adams print in Cole Linden's home. Or a paint-by-number Elvis on black velvet.

She moved hesitantly toward the bedroom, and closed her eyes when she saw Cole's king-sized bed filling the room. Another flat-screen TV perched on a heavy dresser, and Sunshine could all too easily picture Cole stretched out watching a late-night movie. Even if she could remove that monstrosity of a bed, where would she put it?

She gave up any thought of taking over the bedroom. It was the couch for her and living out of a suitcase until she kicked this interloper to the curb.

Exhausted more from the events of the past few weeks than today's traveling, unwelcome tears pricked her eyes and she bit her lip, willing herself not to cry. She hadn't broken down when Greg destroyed her dreams and there was no way she'd start now. There had to be a way out of this mess.

She crossed to the kitchen, opened cabinets until she found a glass and filled it from the tap when she couldn't find any filtered water in the refrigerator. As she surveyed the apartment, she saw a door she hadn't noticed before—another heavy steel door like the one she'd entered through. When she pulled it open, she found herself at the back of the building.

Sunshine gasped. Instead of concrete and a dumpster or two, she found herself stepping out onto a compact deck. It was edged with boxes where small lettuces and a couple of young tomato plants were flourishing in the warm, early summer weather. That wasn't what caught her attention, however. Beyond the deck, just like in the photograph near Cole's dinner table, a vacant lot sloped down, bordered on the far end by two apartment buildings. Behind them stood an old factory and she caught a glint of train tracks in the distance. Had Cole taken the photograph from right here on his back porch?

She stood, dumbfounded, until Cole's very masculine voice sounded behind her. "Finding everything you need?"

She jumped, but didn't turn around. "Just getting the lay of the land." She wouldn't acknowledge her admiration of his photography skills yet, if indeed it was him who'd taken the shot.

She suppressed a shiver at his closeness. She wished she had worn something more modest or business-like, not flowy and feminine, but that was her style and she hadn't thought to change it. She hadn't known she'd face an adversary like Cole.

He took a position next to her and surveyed the scene before them. "I thought you were going to move my furniture." His tone was hard. No-nonsense. He was better at this than she was.

"I don't think I can move your bed."

When his silence stretched out, she finally looked over her shoulder at him.

To her chagrin, a sardonic smile turned up the corner of his mouth. A very sexy smile. "You could always join me in it."

Really? He was going there? Sunshine weighed the benefits of kicking him in the nuts, but visions of his pack of gun-crazy cronies coming after her restrained the impulse.

"I'll take the couch."

"Suit yourself." He moved back inside and she

trailed him into the kitchen, not knowing what else to do. He opened a cabinet and to her horror pulled out a stick of beef jerky. He pulled off a corner of the wrapper with his teeth and began to unwrap it.

"You're going to eat that?" Her stomach cramped just looking at the plastic-looking substance. That stick of gunk had once had a heart and lungs and feelings…

He paused a moment, looked it over and took a bite. Sunshine felt faint. "Yep."

"Do you know what's in it?" She clutched a chair back for support as he raised it to his mouth again. What a barbarian. He looked the part, she noticed, with his muscled torso filling out his T-shirt and camouflage pants. He even wore army boots. She shivered, picturing him with ammunition belts slung crosswise over his shoulders, a flak helmet on his head and a weapon in his hands. She was revolted by the image.

And strangely turned on.

"I bet you're going to tell me." He leaned against the counter, and Sunshine blinked. Tell him? Tell him what?

"About what I'm eating," he prompted.

She dug her fingernails into the wood of the chair. She had to stop focusing on this man's hands and shoulders and focus on the fact that she wasn't going to have a bed for the next four months unless she persuaded him to get the hell out of her apartment.

"Not only are you eating some poor defenseless animal, you are also filling your body with chemicals and preservatives guaranteed to destroy your liver and your immune system and take years off your life. Which you deserve," she added, "for not packing up your stuff and leaving right now."

"Imagine that." He took another bite.

Her stomach recoiled. How could he put that toxic waste into his mouth? And how was she supposed to survive with carrion in her kitchen? "This isn't going to work."

"Glad you finally figured that out. Here's your sixty bucks." He stuck the jerky in his mouth, pulled his wallet out of his pocket and made a show of counting out three twenties.

She stifled a growl. "I didn't say I was going anywhere."

"Well, I know I'm not leaving."

She wanted to slap his handsome face. She doubted that would be a good start to their living or working arrangement, however. And besides, Kate was working on a solution. Kate would fix everything.

She hoped.

Counting silently to ten, she faced the man whose existence was the proverbial fly in the ointment of her happiness. "Fine. I'm going out for several hours. When I get back I'll get settled in. I would prefer some time alone while I do that. Do you think that's possible?"

His shit-eating grin stretched wider. "Anything's possible, Sunshine."

THIRTY MINUTES LATER Sunshine sat at a metal table in the deli section of a supermarket, picking at a three-bean salad she couldn't eat. Her throat was too thick with unshed tears to swallow it down, and even if she managed it, her stomach was tied in knots. Only one day in her life had been worse than this one—the day Greg kicked her out of their apartment, out of the restaurant and out of his life. She'd felt just like this, as a matter of fact—like the rug had been pulled right out from under her feet. She'd assumed giving Greg money to pay for renovations and buy supplies meant they shared ownership of Chez Rosetta. She'd assumed when she moved in with Greg it was as good as being engaged. When her parents asked where the ring was, she'd berated them for their old-fashioned attitudes. "Do you two have some kind of contract for that business of yours?" her father had asked and she'd laughed his question off.

She'd been so stupid.

Now she'd done it again—assumed that when Aunt Cecily said she'd left her a restaurant, she'd meant a real restaurant, not some empty shell inside a shooting gallery. And she'd assumed the apartment she inherited would be hers—not a shared situation with a lunatic.

A hot, gorgeous, capable… sarcastic, barbaric, thief of a lunatic.

She dropped her fork onto her plastic tray and pushed her food aside. Face it, she was totally screwed. She might as well give up and go home. Her parents wouldn't mind if she moved back into her old bedroom.

No.

She was not going to go crying to her parents just

because she was having a bad day. Plenty of people were way worse off. She had her health, her strength, a little money in her pocket, a rent-free situation for her restaurant and a place to live. Sunshine lifted her chin. She'd focus on the future. In four short months, she'd have everything she ever wanted. As long as her restaurant made more money than Cole's rifle-range.

Her thoughts flashed to the man. What had Cecily been thinking, setting her up in a situation like this? She narrowed her eyes. Cecily hadn't been trying to play matchmaker, had she?

Oh, for heaven's sake. She stood up, disposed of her trash and left the market, heading for a furniture store she'd seen a block down the road. Cole could take a flying leap off a very tall building for all she cared.

Several hours later, thoroughly exhausted, she was back in a cab. Decorating an empty apartment would have been easy and fun. Figuring out how to squeeze her things into the tiny box she had to share with Cole was a complete nightmare.

She didn't even want to think about how she'd manage to run a restaurant in the reception area of that travesty of a rifle range.

To HIS CHAGRIN, Cole found himself watching the street outside the rifle range for Sunshine's return later that afternoon. An image stuck in his mind no matter how hard he tried to turn his thoughts to something else—Sunshine's face when Abe the Lawyer began to explain the meaning of her aunt's will. He'd been able to tell the exact moment when she realized the building and the apartment weren't hers, because a look of sheer defeat had twisted her beautiful features before she could school them into outrage.

He didn't like seeing that kind of pain on Sunshine's face, but he told himself a little rich girl like her could find a hundred places to house her café. He was the one in a real fix.

"It's gonna take a lot of work to turn this place into a café," Jamie said, waving an arm at the waiting room. Usually he and the rest of the men would be long gone by now back to work, but evidently they were as curious as he was to see how things turned out.

Cole had been thinking the same thing. There was a kitchen of sorts here behind the counter, but little else. How serious was Sunshine about opening a restaurant? She hadn't even checked the place out before rushing off to shop. Typical rich girl. He hadn't used the stove in here for years. The fridge held bottles of water and soda he sold to his patrons for a buck a pop. The cabinets were mostly empty except for the oil, cleaning cloths and tools he used to repair any firearms that needed it.

"Never gonna pass a health inspection," Rob said.

"Got a broom?" Jamie stood up.

"What for?"

"To sweep, idiot. When's the last time you cleaned this place?"

Cole stared at him in surprise. Why would the cowboy want to help…?

Clarity hit him like a thunderclap. Jamie had set his sights on Sunshine, and why not? She was a beautiful woman. New to the area.

Single.

He pressed down the anger that swirled up within him at the thought of Jamie making a play for her. Jamie could have Sunshine—it wasn't like Cole needed a fling with a hothouse flower like her. Without a word he fetched the push-broom he used to sweep the range and handed it to Jamie. Jamie leaned it against the wall and began to stack the plastic chairs that lined the room.

"This place is a little rough around the edges," Ethan ventured, surveying the small space.

"It's a dump," Cole said. "Once she takes a good look around she'll turn tail and run."

"Does the stove work?" Ethan got up from his chair so Jamie could stack it, sauntered over to the counter and peered behind him toward the old range.

"Beats me," Cole said. "I don't think I've ever tried it."

"Who the hell puts a kitchen in a rifle range, any-how?" Rob said, coming over to join them.

"I think it was a bowling alley at some point. Come on back." Cole waved them around the counter, and Rob and Ethan both came into the area behind it to inspect the tiny kitchen. Ethan shifted some paperwork off the burners, twisted a dial, and when nothing happened turned it off again and bent to look behind the stove.

"Probably isn't even hooked up. You'll have to call

the gas company."

"She'll have to call the gas company."

"Better get this stuff cleared away," Rob said and started moving clipboards, receipts, tools and more paperwork off the kitchen counters.

"Hey! Stop screwing around with that, you'll mess up my system."

"What system?" Rob kept going. "Time you cleaned up your act anyway. You can never find anything the way you run this place."

What the hell? Had Rob decided to throw his hat in the ring, too? Rob had always been one for the ladies and currently he didn't have a girlfriend. Ethan did, however. His intentions toward Sunshine had better be platonic.

He noticed Cab had stood up, too, and was pacing off the dimensions of the room. Was he calculating how many tables would fit? Cole couldn't believe these turncoats. One look at Sunshine's lithe body and pretty face and they were ready to burn a trail through his rifle range like Sherman on his way to Atlanta.

Jamie kept stacking chairs. Rob and Ethan faced Cole, waiting. Holt cackled softly in his corner of the waiting room. "Hope she makes a good cup of coffee. Your brew tastes like pig slops."

"That's it. Everyone out!" For good measure he pointed at the door. "You heard me—go on! Bunch of traitors."

"But—"

"Now. I've got work to do."

Jamie let go of a chair and it fell to the ground with a metallic thud. The others hesitated, then retreated toward the door. "All right, man. See you soon," Rob said. The four younger men filed out onto the sidewalk and dispersed toward their cars. Holt took a while longer to unfold himself from his chair.

"I've got a little advice for you, Cole," he said when he finally managed to straighten up. "Might sound familiar."

"Oh yeah, what's that?" He tried to keep his voice even. He had a lot of respect for his father's old friend, a hardened rancher from one of the oldest families in town.

"If you want to catch a rabbit, don't bait your trap with a bear."

"I've never heard that saying, old man."

"Then use your head and figure it out. You don't need to fight that little girl to get what you want. That's what she's expecting you to do, and if you fight, she'll fight back." He shook his head. "Kill her with kindness. Let her have her café. Hell, put on an apron and flip the burgers for her."

"She's a vegetarian," Cole said. Holt wasn't making any sense at all.

"Then flip the tofu. Whatever it takes. Look around you—who the hell is going to come to eat at a rifle range? She'll spend her money, work herself silly and fall flat on her face." Holt jabbed him in the shoulder with a bony finger. "And then she'll take your sixty bucks and go back where she came from. Or not." He grinned.

"What do you mean, *or not?*"

"Maybe you'll convince her to stay."

Holt left without another word, leaving Cole to stare after him with his mouth hanging open. He wasn't going to convince Sunshine to stay. He was going to salute her backside with a bottle of beer as she walked out the door. Whatever Cecily thought, Sunshine wasn't his type.

But the more he thought about it, the more he realized Holt was right about one thing. She was just the type to settle in for a good fight if he provoked her. Far better to help her along to her own demise. He ducked under the counter, grabbed the broom and got to work.

Chapter Three

A<small>N HOUR LATER</small> he had made substantial progress. He'd swept the floor and knocked down the cobwebs within easy reach. He'd found a pail and squeegee and cleaned the inside of the plate glass window. Now he was mopping the floor. Cole took a break to swig a pop and admire the fruit of his labor. Even if the benefits of it would accrue to a woman who stood to steal his father's shooting range out from under him, he was enough of a man to feel the pride of accomplishment in his work.

"What the hell are you doing?"

The angry female voice froze him in place.

The front door slammed and Sunshine walked in, laden down with bags and boxes. Cleaning supplies, Cole realized.

"I said, what the fuck are you doing?" She dropped everything on the damp floor where he had just mopped and stared at him, pale with anger. She was still beautiful, Cole thought, her blonde hair framing her face, her breasts heaving with each furious breath, but she looked ready to flay him alive and roast him in her still-filthy oven.

"Just thought I'd lend a hand," Cole said cautiously.

"Lend a hand? Without asking? How do you know what I want done in here? Huh? It's my building, my café—I don't need anyone's help, certainly not yours. What were you thinking coming into my space without permission, rattling around and... and..."

"Mopping the floor?" Cole supplied.

"Mopping the floor!" Sunshine strode over to him and yanked the mop out of his hand. "I didn't say you could mop my floor." She jabbed a finger into his chest, "You might think that just because you've been a tenant here for a few years that you own the place, but..."

"Twenty years."

"What?" She stopped mid-sentence and blinked at him.

"Twenty years. My father owned the rifle range before I did. He's the one who sold the building to Cecily. We've been in business here twenty years."

She tightened her lips and when she spoke again, her voice was quietly furious. "You may think you own the place because you've been a tenant for twenty years, but you are wrong. I own this building. I intend to live and work here for the next four months, and then I will kick you out on your ass. From now on stay on your side of the room."

Cole waited long enough for a deep, highly uncomfortable silence to settle over them before he turned around and quietly walked through the door into the rifle range. Inside, he was fuming, but he was glad he'd managed to keep a handle on his temper. She was the one who had to be embarrassed now when she looked around and realized all he'd done was help.

SUNSHINE'S ARM ACHED and her eyelids drooped. She was standing on top of the back counter, cleaning out the cabinets in the kitchen area. She deeply regretted that there was no back room in this place except for the shooting range itself. The kitchen was wide open to the front of the café, so she couldn't even daydream about sleeping here on a regular basis instead of in the apartment. Besides, that would probably violate the terms of the will, and she wasn't going to do anything that might result in Cole buying the building for a lousy sixty bucks.

She crouched down and jumped off the counter, landing unsteadily on the linoleum floor. She was exhausted and she hadn't eaten any dinner. Hardly any lunch, either, she thought, remembering the bean salad she'd thrown away. Time to face the music. She was so embarrassed by her behavior this afternoon. How could she have blown up at Cole when all he'd done was clean up his mess? It was amazing he'd go to the trouble in the first place. If she'd been in his place she'd be shoveling manure into the store, not rolling up her sleeves and mopping the floor.

At first she'd convinced herself that it was some sort of trick and she'd worked tensely, waiting to discover the joke. After an hour had passed, however, she had to admit that all he'd done was clean her floor. Now she felt like a jackass.

Several of Cole's clients had wandered through and she'd directed them into the back. They'd taken a moment to check out her progress—or maybe they were checking her out, she wasn't sure—but they didn't seem to think it strange that they might have to find their own way through the rear door into the range without Cole there to greet them. Now and then she heard bursts of male laughter and she wondered if she was the topic of conversation. She hoped Cole wasn't relaying her fit of hysterics when she caught him cleaning up, but from the amused glances one or two sent her way when they exited the range again, she thought he might be.

The gunfire that erupted now and then put her on edge. She had no experience with firearms. It was unnerving to think that men with loaded weapons were just feet away from her, but somehow even though she disliked the man, she trusted Cole to run a safe operation.

She rubbed the small of her back where it ached from the unaccustomed work she'd been doing, her mind traveling back to the scene she'd made. Cole had done a terrific job on the parts of the store he'd cleaned, and saved her some work, and then she'd burst in like a harpy, shrieking and swearing at him. Her cheeks burned just thinking about it. It was Greg's voice she'd heard in her ear when she'd walked in and saw Cole working. "It's my restaurant, Sunshine. You like to pretend to work here, but we all know you're just play-acting. You and your associate degree. You're not a real chef. You're just a cook. You don't know the first thing about running the place."

The last thing she needed was another man taking over her café and telling her what to do. Still, maybe that wasn't what Cole had intended. Maybe he was just being nice.

She put away the cleaning supplies and hesitated. It was time to return to the apartment, but how should she behave when she saw Cole again? Should she apologize, or assume that he'd try to undercut her at some point and so deserved to be yelled at?

She glanced at the time. It was late, but not that late. Kate would be up. All afternoon and evening she'd told herself she wouldn't run to her friend with yet another sob story, but she needed to tell someone about her crazy day, and who else but Kate would pick up the phone at this hour?

"Good, he didn't shoot you yet." Kate's voice rang out over the phone as confidently as usual when she answered, and Sunshine sighed, wishing she had her friend's stamina.

"You're not still at work, are you?" she asked. She could swear she heard a murmur of voices in the background.

"I'm on a date, actually."

"A date?" Kate hadn't mentioned anyone new, although Sunshine realized she hadn't given her friend much of a chance to talk about herself these past few weeks.

"Yes, so talk fast."

"It's not important. Just been a rough day."

"I'm not surprised." But Kate sounded more distracted than usual. Sunshine had hoped to give her a blow-by-blow description of what had happened, but that obviously wasn't going to work. "It's Cole Linden. He's not going to go away easily."

"Mm-hmm."

"He won't move his stuff. He expects me to sleep on the couch." Sunshine warmed to her theme. "He's a carnivore, too. And I think he might have been in the military."

"That's nice."

Sunshine frowned. Nice? Was Kate even listening to her?

"I don't think—"

Kate interrupted her. "Hold on a minute." Her voice suddenly muffled, as if she'd covered the phone with her hand. "Just a friend," Sunshine heard her say. "Major drama, as usual."

Kate came back. "I'm working on that contract of yours, so just sit tight. I'll figure out how to get you out of this mess."

But Sunshine hardly heard her. Her cheeks felt hot, but the rest of her felt cold. She stood frozen in place. Was that how Kate thought of her—as a drama queen? She forced herself to say, "Thanks. I appreciate it. I'll let you go."

"Let's talk tomorrow." Kate rang off and Sunshine stared at her phone, still reeling. It was true she used

Kate as a sounding board, but Kate used her for the same purpose, didn't she? Sunshine thought back over their conversations. Maybe not. Kate was the one who listened and gave advice. She rarely had any problems to sort out. Maybe this new boyfriend of hers would dump her. Then *she* could be the drama queen.

When she let herself into the apartment a few minutes later, however, Sunshine was still numb with shock. She'd never thought of herself as overdramatic, but maybe she'd been fooling herself. She's always leaned on Kate to be the practical one—a balance to her more creative, free-spirited ways. Maybe there was no balance, however. Maybe she was a fuck-up, and Kate the good friend that saved her from herself over and over again.

She was grateful for the darkness that greeted her when she opened the door. Maybe she wouldn't have to say anything at all to Cole tonight. It looked like he'd already gone to bed. If she was quiet enough not to wake him, she could put off an encounter until morning. By then she'd be able to pull herself together.

She cleaned up in the bathroom, taking a quick shower and filching one of Cole's towels to dry off with. She'd left her toothbrush in here earlier, so at least she could clean her teeth. Once prepped for bed, she prepared to tip-toe to the couch, but as she put her hand on the bathroom doorknob to open it, a muffled blast of music split the quiet of the apartment and she winced when she realized its source—her cell-phone.

She dashed out of the bathroom for her purse, unclasped it and fished around until she found her phone.

"Kate?"

"Could that be any louder?" Cole called from his bedroom.

Sunshine cringed, all too aware she was still wrapped in his towel. "Sorry!" She held the phone to her ear. "Hello?"

"It's about time."

Greg. Shit. "I can't talk right now."

"Why not? Why are you whispering?" It was clear he'd been drinking and Sunshine braced herself for an unpleasant conversation. All of Greg's irritating qualities grew particularly irritating when he drank.

"Because someone's sleeping in the next room."

"I'm not sleeping," Cole said, much closer this time. She turned around to find him leaning against the doorframe wearing nothing but boxer briefs. Her gaze dipped then snapped back up to his face.

"Who's sleeping in the next room? Where the fuck are you, Sunshine? I hired a new manager and I need the extra set of keys. How many times do I have to tell you to give them back?"

"Stop yelling at me!" Sunshine bit her lip. "Look, it's the middle of the night. I don't have them, so leave me alone."

"Bullshit. I'm not paying for a locksmith to come and change the locks just because you're too lazy to return them."

"Everything all right?" Cole straightened, and she had to force herself to look at his face rather than ogle the broad expanse of his chest or his impressive biceps. His hair was mussed and standing on end, but he looked concerned rather than angry.

"Who's that? Found yourself a new sugar daddy already? You'll spread your legs to any rising star who'll let you come along for the ride, won't you?"

"Fuck off, Greg."

"I want my keys!"

"I don't have your…"

Cole stepped forward and took the phone from her hand.

"Listen, asshole—Sunshine doesn't want to talk to you. Call here again and I'll track you down, tear you limb from limb and bury your body parts in nine separate states. Got it?" He cut the call and turned the phone's sound off before handing it back to her.

"That was my ex-fiancé," she said.

Cole snorted. "Why am I not surprised?"

After Cole disappeared back into his room, Sunshine slipped into the bathroom, changed into a short nighty, and climbed gratefully into her makeshift bed. This had been one of the worst days of her life and Greg's obnoxious behavior was just the icing on the cake. Thank God Cole had been here to deal with him, because if she'd had to talk to him for one more minute she would have dissolved into a screaming mess. She shivered with distaste.

She settled on the couch and pulled a light sheet up around her shoulders, needing the comfort of covers even though the night was warm. She had once been so in love with Greg and he'd been in love with her. When had that changed?

When her savings had begun to run out.

Greg assumed because her family was rich she had access to a never-ending supply of money, and she supposed in a way he was right. If she needed something and asked her parents for it, most likely they would help her out. What Greg didn't understand, however, was that she'd been raised not to ask except in the case of the direst emergency. She was proud she'd managed to save enough money from her jobs in high school and college to have a sizeable bank account by the time she'd met Greg. She'd applied for a sous chef position at his newly opened restaurant and soon she'd proven her worth in every aspect of the business. When they began to date, and he confessed he was short on funds for some upgrades, she'd been pleased to become his partner. They'd run the restaurant together for over a year.

Of course, now she saw the truth. She was young, cute and rich, and he'd used all those attributes to his advantage. When she ceased being an asset, in the most monetary sense of the word, he'd discarded her.

Well, screw him. She didn't need Greg or his stupid restaurant. She had everything she needed right here.

Doubt assailed her when she thought of the ramshackle, empty space that would soon house her café. Was she kidding herself? What if Greg was right? What if she screwed this up, too?

She threw back the covers and tip-toed into the

kitchen. It was obvious she wouldn't sleep tonight, so she might as well start making plans. She needed to open her café sooner rather than later—before her dwindling supply of cash ran out. She made herself a cup of tea and then sat at the scrubbed wooden table with a tablet of paper and a pen in front of her. As the minutes ticked by, however, she found herself doodling Cole's name instead of a list of supplies she needed to buy.

Cole was handsome, not in a movie-star kind of way, but in a manly, I-know-what-I'm-doing kind of way. Big and strong and masculine; just the way she liked them. Greg had been cute enough, but Cole filled out his jeans and t-shirt in a way Greg never could. He was easy in his skin and she had the feeling he could change a tire, or fix a dishwasher—things Greg would have to hire someone else to do. She'd noticed Cole's hands, earlier—large, strong, hands capable of doing all sorts of things.

Sunshine groaned. This was getting her nowhere except hot and bothered with no relief in sight. She tore off the top sheet of paper, crumpled it up and threw it in the trash, then crossed the room to the back door and let herself out onto the deck. There was little traffic at this late hour in the small town, but enough light shone from streetlights to illuminate the meadow that sloped away from her. She shivered a little in the cool air, suddenly lonelier than she could ever remember being. Greg was gone. Not the asshole who called a short time ago to yell at her, but the ideal Greg she'd created in her mind and fallen in love with. Would she ever believe in love again?

Could someone else ease the ache in her heart? And the ache between her legs?

Truth be told she missed sex almost as much as she missed the fantasy relationship she thought she had with Greg. He might be an asshole, but at least he'd touched her, held her and had enough basic chivalry to make sure she'd shared his pleasure in making love.

The six weeks since they'd broken up seemed to stretch into months. She knew she was pretty in a girl-next-door sort of way. She knew she'd have other boyfriends in the future. Knew it in her head, anyway.

Her bruised, broken, stomped-on heart said something different. After all, Kate and Greg, the two people who knew her the best, didn't find her all that compelling. Maybe they were right. Maybe she was a drama queen. Maybe she was unlovable.

Maybe she'd be alone forever.

She didn't hear the door open behind her, so when Cole touched her back, Sunshine jumped.

"It's just me," he said in a low, husky voice. "You okay?"

Sunshine bowed her head, tears pricking her eyes at this unlooked for kindness. Had Greg ever asked her if she was okay?

"I'm fine. It's just..." To her horror, tears spilled down her cheeks and the pain in her throat grew to an enormous lump that threatened to choke her until she let out a great gasp of sadness.

Cole pulled her into his arms, one hand at the small of her back, the other cradling her head, and she leaned against him, sobbing all the tears she'd held in for so long. She wanted to push away, run inside, dive under her covers, and hide from him for the remainder of her days, but she couldn't have moved for the world. As long as he held her she could push back the chasm of loneliness that threatened to pull her in for all eternity. Just for a minute she didn't have to face the future alone.

Chapter Four

I F THE GUYS could see him now.

Cole was too stunned to think anything more coherent. When he'd heard Sunshine get up from the couch again, he'd assumed she'd needed to use the washroom, but then the back door had opened, and he'd decided he needed to investigate. When he'd spotted her out on the deck in that flimsy shortie nightgown, all rational thought had flown from his head and instinct kicked in. As soon as he'd taken her into his arms he'd been lost.

Now her breasts pressed against his bare chest, her nipples, hard in the cool night air, all too evident through the thin material covering them. His right hand was an inch above her ass and only the strongest effort kept it from straying southward. Her tears wet his shoulder and her breath was hot against his throat.

And he was getting hard.

There was no stopping it, and Cole was sure any second Sunshine would fling herself away from him in disgust and make a beeline for her couch, but she didn't. Instead, she let out a soft moan that was nearly his undoing and wrapped her arms around his neck.

Cole's surprise stopped him momentarily, but within the space of seconds his decidedly male instincts kicked in with a vengeance. He tightened his arms around her small, curvy body, and bent down to cover her mouth with his own.

She met him kiss for kiss, her lips parting to allow his tongue entrance, and when he pulled her closer, she didn't resist. In fact, she leaned into him. Cole stifled a groan, slid a hand down to caress her bottom.

Sunshine gasped and pulled away. "What are you doing?"

"Enjoying what you're offering me."

"I'm not… offering you anything!"

Back to square one. Cole sighed, but didn't argue. "I'm heading back to bed. You can join me if you like. Or not. It's your call."

"You won't win by seducing me. I'm not that easy." She was furious and he'd bet she was blushing too, but he couldn't see that kind of detail in the dim light.

"See you in the morning, Sunshine."

He escaped to his bedroom, glad he at least had enough common sense to know this couldn't end well.

But it was a long time before he fell asleep.

SUNSHINE TOSSED AND turned for hours, finally falling asleep just as dawn broke and fingers of light slipped under the curtains. When Cole came through the room at seven-thirty, she groaned and covered her head with her pillow.

"Rise and shine. Don't you have a restaurant to run?"

"Go away." She didn't want to see the man— definitely not like this. Unshowered, her eyes swollen from lack of sleep. Plus she couldn't help remembering their embrace last night.

Their kiss.

She buried her head deeper under the pillow. What was she going to do now? Why had she let him see her weakness—her sorrow over losing Greg? Now he'd make fun of her for it. He'd probably tell all his friends about kissing her.

Although if she was honest, it had been nice. More than nice. Cole was muscular and handsome, and his attentions had made her feel beautiful... for a minute, until he'd tried to grab her ass and she'd realized just what he was after—a quick roll in the hay he could use to torment and humiliate her until she left town and he got the building.

No way.

She'd never kiss or touch him again. She sure as hell wouldn't sleep with him, even if the idea was tempting as hell.

She shrieked when Cole suddenly ripped her covers away from her body. Scrambling to her knees, she tried to grab them back but he held them out of reach. He laughed down at her and she realized the disadvantage he had her in. He was fully dressed in jeans and a T-shirt. She wore practically nothing at all.

"Breakfast in five minutes. Want the shower?" He

didn't wait for an answer. He dumped her covers in the easy chair across the room and headed back to the kitchen. A minute later she heard the clatter of dishes and silverware and Cole's low, warm voice singing snatches of country and western songs.

Damn him. Why did he have to be a morning person? She never had been, despite her name. Too late now to try to get more sleep, though. She stood up wearily and trudged to the bathroom. A shower revived her some, and once she'd located her hair products in her bag and gotten dressed in a slightly wrinkled set of clothes, she felt more like herself. The dining room table was set for two people with a vase of flowers in the middle when she came back out of the bathroom. Cole approached it with two full plates in his hand. "Take a seat." He deposited one plate in front of her and set the other on the opposite side of the table.

"Are you always this chipper?" She sat down, eyeing the flowers suspiciously.

"Pretty much. Especially when a beautiful woman's eating breakfast with me." He flashed her a grin she figured got him a lot of female attention. "Plus today is the start of my annual Six Shooters and Six Packs competition."

"Do I even want to know what that is?"

"Probably not," Cole said cheerfully. "But I'll tell you anyway. It's a month-long competition. I have ten kinds of targets available at the range. To make things more interesting," he added when he saw her confused expression. "Any time one of my regulars comes in he can choose one to shoot at and try to improve his score. At the end of the month I add up each shooter's top scores for all ten kinds of targets. The best one overall wins a six pack of beer every week for the next year. The guys love it. Really gets their competitive spirit flowing." He looked very satisfied at that thought.

Sunshine thought it sounded barbaric. "So you're mixing booze and shooting? Are you nuts?"

"The booze comes after the shooting." Cole wasn't fazed. "So be prepared for lots of foot traffic this month."

"Your customers better be prepared to keep out of my way while I renovate," she countered.

"Renovate?" Cole frowned. "Who said anything about renovating?"

"I did. I want my restaurant running by the end of the month."

Chapter Five

COLE GRIMACED. HE didn't want a restaurant running at all—not in his gun club. Even the most dedicated shooter could be distracted by a decent hamburger or steak. If Sunshine set out a good feed, he might lose half his clientele. If she got a liquor license, he'd lose the rest.

"How much money do you plan to spend on the renovation?"

"That's my business." But she looked uncomfortable and Cole's spirits picked up. If she didn't have much money to spruce up the place, she'd have trouble attracting customers. It wasn't like the range was on a thoroughfare, after all.

"Are you planning to—"

"Like I said, it's my business. Which I'll go attend to right now." She threw down her fork and stood up. Cole noticed she'd barely eaten a single pancake.

"Aren't you hungry?"

"You used milk in those pancakes. That's cruel to the cows."

Cruel to the cows? Cole figured it would be a lot crueler not to milk them. Had she ever seen a full udder? He stabbed her pancakes and transferred them to his own plate. No sense wasting them.

A half-hour later he stood in the doorway of the waiting room. Or what used to be his waiting room. The chairs were now stacked on the sidewalk. All the paperwork that had been piled on the counter was gone. So were the rest of his belongings.

"Hey!" He strode inside and spotted a lopsided stack of his things. "You can't just—"

"You should be ashamed of yourself." Sunshine popped up behind the counter and waved a rag in his direction that was covered with a greasy smudge of dirt and grime. "Have you ever wiped down this counter? Or anything in this place? By the way, the bathroom needs to be stripped down to the studs. I've never seen anything so disgusting."

Cole frowned. "This ain't my grandmother's parlor."

"No. It's a cess pool. Worse than a cess pool. Has your mother ever been in here?"

"No, she hasn't." His temper flared. "My mother is dead."

Sunshine stood up. She let the rag fall. "I'm sorry. I shouldn't have said that."

"No, you shouldn't. And you should remember you're in someone's place of business."

"Humph." She made a face. "I'd hardly call this a place of business. More like a disaster area." She walked over to the till that stood at one end of the counter. "This dinosaur has to go."

"That's my cash register." He came to stand in front of it.

"Where's mine supposed to go?"

"I don't know. Over there?" He pointed to the other end of the long, wooden span.

She shook her head. "That's not going to work. We need a clear demarcation of our two spaces." She paced into the waiting area and pointed to the door. "Your customers can enter here and walk down this corridor." She dragged her foot along the floor as if drawing a line with it, indicating a three-foot-wide strip of flooring that led to the door into the range. "The rest of this front room, including the counter and everything behind it is for my café."

"How the hell do you figure that?"

"Half this entire building is mine. We can either divide it up with the front being mine and the back yours, or if you want to share my space up front, then I'll take half your shooting range. I could fit a lot of tables in there."

Cole spluttered. "You can't do that." Time for a tactical retreat. He scanned the front room. "I suppose I could build myself a check-in counter right in front of the door to the range."

She shrugged. "That would work. Thank you."

Cole gathered his papers together, deposited them on the floor on his side and found a tape measure. Soon he had the dimensions for the counter he needed to build. It was a damned nuisance, but the thought of Sunshine intruding into the inner sanctum of his rifle range was even worse.

By midmorning he'd hacked together a makeshift stand, complete with shelves on the back side for all his files and supplies. It wasn't fancy, and it wasn't big, but it would do. Sunshine was still cleaning up a storm. It had taken her more than an hour to scrub down the long counter until she was satisfied with it. Then she'd done the same for the shelves beneath it. Now she was working on the old stove. Cole figured if she had any money to spend she'd replace the beast, so she must be as pinched for cash as he was.

"You'll need to buy your own register, you know," he said, unscrewing the old one from the main counter.

"I know." She didn't sound happy about it.

"Maybe you can find a used one." He clamped his mouth shut before he could offer her any more good advice. The last thing he needed was to help her win.

"Hey Cole, hey Sunshine." Jamie walked in and surveyed the place. "Some big changes in the works, huh?"

"Guess so," Cole said. Sunshine nodded at Jamie but said nothing. Cole wondered if she was afraid of the men who came into the range. Maybe they were a rougher crowd than she was used to. If that was the case, she must hang out with some refined company. Jamie and the rest of them were simply ranchers—men who worked with their hands for a living. Nothing too rough about that.

"Anything I can do to help?"

Cole realized Jamie was making the offer to Sunshine, not him. The traitor.

Sunshine looked up. Realized Jamie was speaking to her. "Not right now, thanks."

"You just say the word if you think of anything. That's what neighbors do here; we pitch in."

Sunshine looked around the room and Cole could see her considering this. Before she could put Jamie to work, he quickly said, "Ready to sign up for the Six-shooters and Six Packs contest, Jamie?"

"You bet I am." He kept his gaze on Sunshine, though. "Just holler if you need me, Sunshine. Here. I'll write down my number." He did so on a scrap of paper and pushed it across the counter to her. She looked up at him through her lashes and Cole's ire rose. She was flirting with Jamie. Right in front of him.

Cole managed to steer the man toward the range and shoved a target into his hand. "Better go get started."

He'd no sooner escorted Jamie into the range area than Ethan showed up. He was already passing Sunshine a business card when Cole came back into the front room. "Call me any time, day or night," he was saying to her. "I know Lacey would like to meet you sometime."

Like hell she would, Cole thought. He marched over and snatched the card off the counter. "Do you not understand that if Sunshine succeeds there won't be any more rifle range?"

"Sunshine wouldn't shut down the range," Ethan protested. "She's too nice to do something like that, right?"

Sunshine shrugged. "I could use some help cleaning that refrigerator."

"Sure thing. Where's the—ouch!"

Cole raised his arm to swipe Ethan again. "Get in back and start shooting. That's an order."

"Hell, Cole, what kind of business are you running? You can't hit your customers."

"Watch me." He raised his arm again and Ethan moved past him, chuckling.

"Someone's mighty touchy this morning. Had trouble sleeping last night, Cole? Did a certain pretty lady keep you up?" He disappeared into the back. Sunshine glared at Cole.

"You'd better not say a word to anyone about what happened last night. I was sad, that's all there was to it."

"Calm down, sweetheart. I wouldn't spoil my reputation by admitting I'd kissed you. People would talk." He leered at her.

She threw the dirty rag at him.

"Am I interrupting something?"

Cole turned to find Rob in the doorway.

"Is Cole bothering you, honey?" Rob continued as he came across the room. "He has a bad habit of not knowing where he isn't wanted." He shoved Cole aside and leaned against the counter. He fished a slip of paper out of his pocket and put it into Sunshine's hand, curving her fingers over it. "That's my number. You want anything... and I mean anything... you give me a call."

She flicked a glance at Cole and a devilish smile

curved her mouth. She folded the paper twice and slid it into her bra. "I'll do that." Leaning forward across the counter, she gave Rob—and Cole—an eyeful of cleavage. "I don't suppose you'd run out to the local supermarket and buy me some organic coffee?"

"Hell, yeah." Rob was halfway to the door before she finished speaking. Cole had to run to catch up with him.

"You do that and you're banned from the range for life."

"That ain't—"

"For life." Cole waited for that to sink in. "Jamie and Ethan are already in back winning the Six Shooter and Six Pack contest. Are you gonna get back there or not?"

"Aw, I guess so." Rob winked at Sunshine as he walked on by. "Don't worry, honey. I'll hook you up later."

"Don't think you can set my friends against me," Cole said to Sunshine as soon as Rob disappeared into the back.

"I'm not doing anything."

"Like hell. Flashing those… breasts."

She laughed out loud. "These ol' things? My momma gave them to me and I'll flash them whenever I want." She returned to her cleaning, which was a good thing because it meant she missed the smile which stretched across his face at that preposterous declaration. For a second she'd sounded as sassy as a country girl. Maybe there was hope for her yet.

"Looks good in here," Cab proclaimed as he walked in. "Cole, you should have cleaned the place years ago."

"I clean."

"Huh." Cab didn't sound convinced. "Morning, Sunshine. How's your day going?"

"Just fine."

He ambled closer and handed her a card. Sunshine took it with a sweet smile.

"I'm the local sheriff, just so you know." Cab tipped his hat to her, then took it off. "Anyone bothers you, you tell me about it and I'll take care of it."

Sunshine raised an eyebrow. "Well, there is one man being a real nuisance."

"Oh yeah? Who?"

Cole had a feeling he knew exactly where this was going. "All right. Enough chit chat. Cab, you here for the contest?"

"Give me a minute. Who's bothering you?" When Cab was in sheriff mode he was mighty imposing. Normally Cole didn't figure the man to be much competition with the ladies, but he could see how someone like Sunshine—with her belligerent ex—might be drawn to the big man.

"Well, he's tall," she said. "He's got brown hair. But his most distinguishing characteristic is the enormous ego he's always lugging around."

Cab's mouth twitched. "Oh, yeah? Is he kind of a gun nut? Messy, too?"

"That's him!" She pretended to be surprised. "Does he bother everyone?"

"Pretty much." Cab slapped Cole on the shoulder. Hard. "But he'll keep himself in line, won't he, Cole?"

"He'll do whatever he damned well pleases."

"Cole."

Cole rolled his eyes. "Whatever. Are you here to shoot or to gab, Sheriff?"

"A little of both." He smiled at Sunshine. "Remember—call me if you need help."

"Thank you, Sheriff." She added his card to her collection in her bra and Cole had to shake himself to keep his gaze from lingering on the swell of her breasts. He would love to touch them, to smooth his hands over them...

"Eyes forward," Sunshine snapped.

He jolted out of his reverie, then allowed a slow smile to curve his lips. "Yes, ma'am."

COLE WAS ABSOLUTELY insufferable, Sunshine thought as she got back to scrubbing. It would serve him right if she picked one of his friends to date and flaunted the relationship in front of him on a daily basis. Still, every time she failed to guard her thoughts, it was Cole, not one of the other cowboys, her mind returned to. The way he'd held her last night had her body buzzing with desire. She'd wanted him to do far more than kiss her.

She pushed away the thought. She needed to focus on the restaurant—on whipping it into some kind of shape as soon as possible. Once again she wondered how she'd ended up here—a far cry from the high-end establishment she always thought she'd run.

Of course, she'd always thought she'd take all that money she'd saved during high school and college and spend it on a year traveling around the world, learning from the best of the best—and maybe being hired by one of them. She'd blown all that money on Greg, though, and she'd have to work hard if she ever wanted to save it up again.

It took the remainder of the morning to clean the oven and scrub every inch of the stovetop. By the time noon rolled around she was hungrier than she'd been in months. She figured it was unlikely she'd find any vegan dishes at the local restaurants. Time to visit a grocery store, then whip back to the apartment to cook for herself.

She didn't bother to tell Cole she was leaving. He was still in back with a bunch of regulars who'd trickled in as the morning passed. She ignored them for the most part, flirted with them when she thought it would get Cole's goat, but her mind was firmly on the costs she faced to get her restaurant up and running.

Twenty minutes later she was standing in the vegetable aisle of the local grocery store, surveying her choices. She picked up a zucchini, some garlic and onions, a head of lettuce and other salad vegetables. As she walked through the store, however, there were many things she couldn't find.

"Excuse me," she said to a young woman manning one of the tills some minutes later, "can you tell me where you stock your almond milk?"

"Almond milk?" The woman shot her a funny look.

"I don't think we carry it."

"What about tofu?"

"We had some of that for a while, but no one bought it. You'll have to place a special order."

"Nutritional yeast?"

"Nutritional what?"

Sunshine sighed. "Is your manager here?"

After a rather dispiriting conversation with the manager, Sunshine placed a special order of all the things she needed to cook her normal staples. Today she'd have a simple zucchini burrito with the Thai peanut sauce she was overjoyed to find next to the ketchup.

What this place needed, she decided as she made her way home, was a buying co-op so that people like her could order specialty foods for reasonable prices. She couldn't be the only one in town who wanted more variety in their diet. She'd have to look into starting one, if no one else had already. She might as well, since she'd be ordering food for her restaurant.

When she reached the apartment, she found Cole lunching on a large hamburger and French fries from a fast food chain. The smell permeated the place and turned Sunshine's stomach. She knew asking him to leave wouldn't turn out well, so she opened all the windows and doors instead.

"You're letting in the flies."

"I'm letting out the smell."

"Why would you do that? I love the smell of a hamburger." He took another bite. Sunshine ignored him and headed into the kitchen. She prepped a salad and fried up the zucchini with some of the garlic and onion in a pan she'd found when she hunted around.

"I don't remember giving you permission to use my things," Cole said, bringing his trash to the receptacle under the sink. In the small kitchen he loomed over her.

"If you want I'll buy a second set."

After a long pause he said, "Don't bother. You won't be here long enough to make that necessary."

Sunshine vowed right then and there that she would.

"I'm heading back to the shop." He turned away.

"Fine."

"You coming when you're done?"

She frowned at the question. He almost sounded like he hoped she would. "I need to shop for a few things first."

"Okay." He hesitated behind her. "You know, if circumstances were different…"

She gripped the counter, his words eliciting a slow roil of desire within her. She refused to go there, even though she knew instinctively the kind of magic they could make together. "If circumstances were different you and I would never have met."

Chapter Six

C OLE STRODE BACK to the rifle range as fast as his legs could carry him and didn't notice Holt inside until the old man spoke.

"She's getting to you, isn't she? Don't fall for that."

"She's not getting to me."

"Then what's got you in a tizzy?"

"Having to share my range with that...that...woman!"

Holt chuckled. "I don't suppose she's too pleased either."

"Probably not, but I was here first."

"But Cecily was her aunt. I imagine according to her way of seeing things, you're the interloper."

"You're not helping."

"Tell you what. You shouldn't be worried. It's not like she's going to serve anything any of us want to eat."

Holt had that right. Fried zucchini in a tortilla for lunch? He shuddered at the thought. She'd been horrified by his burger, too. If she planned to only serve vegetarian food at her café, he didn't have to worry that all his customers would defect to eat her food. He glanced at the calendar on his wall. Four short months and he'd own this building outright, which meant every penny could go to paying down the mortgage on the apartments. Who knew? Maybe he wouldn't have to renovate anything for a while and they'd start to make more money.

Cole nodded. "You know what? You're right. I'm going to put her out of my mind."

Holt laughed louder. "Oh, I doubt that." He strolled on past, patting Cole's shoulder as he went. "I doubt that very much."

Cole had to admit Holt was right an hour later. An hour in which Sunshine rarely left his mind, even as he served his clients. Some of his tenants were regulars here, including Scott Preston, who was one of the best marksmen he'd ever met. He arrived around two-thirty, paid his fee and wandered into the range. Cole glanced over toward Sunshine's side of the room. What was she doing all this time? Why hadn't she come back?

He had his answer when the door opened and she staggered in under the weight of a metal cash register. Despite his intentions not to help her one bit, Cole rushed to take it from her arms and set it on the counter. "Where'd you get this?"

"Turned out a business closed on Main Street. The man at the furniture store told me about it. I was able to buy it really cheap. They even gave me the manual." She went back out the door and came in a moment later with a bag. "Plus some register paper and some other odds and ends. They also had a spare table and a couple of chairs. They're delivering them later."

Cole shook his head as he watched her unpack all her finds. A file stand, a receipt book, and other bits that might be handy for a business. If people kept helping Sunshine, he was going to end up a creek without a paddle.

An idea popped into his mind. Maybe he needed to do some shopping himself.

"Watch the place, would you? I'll be back soon."

Without waiting for an answer, he left the building. An hour later, he was nailing his newest purchase up on the wall when Sunshine stalked over to stand behind him. "What on earth is that for?"

He stepped back and surveyed the four foot by six foot white board. "Looks level. I'll be right back." He went out to his truck and retrieved the second white board which he proceeded to hold up next to the first.

"You're taking up an entire wall."

"There are four walls. I'm only taking up part of one. You've got plenty of wall left over for your girlie stuff." He marked where he needed to drill for the screws and got to work.

"What are they for?" she hollered over the sound of his drill.

"Scorekeeping. People like to know who's winning the Six-shooters and Six Pack contest. I figured I'd make the scores public this year."

"I should have guessed." She turned to go, but stopped when Jamie walked out of the range.

"Hi, Sunshine. How's it going?"

"Fine."

"Hey, what are these?" Jamie came to survey the white boards. Cole fished a brand-new marker out of a shopping bag, and wrote Jamie's name at the top of the left board. He wrote the name of each target across the top of the board and wrote in Jamie's scores as he reported them. "I like this much better than the old way. They look good, too. Kind of liven up the place."

"I think so, too." Cole smirked at Sunshine. Maybe next he'd find some trophies to hand on the wall. A few deer. Maybe a lynx. His expression fell, however, when Jamie turned around and announced, "You probably don't know how to shoot, do you, Sunshine? I could teach you. You should learn if you're going to be around firearms all day."

"That's a lousy idea." Cole stated, but backtracked when Jamie looked at him in surprise. "I mean, Sunshine isn't interested in shooting. She told me that herself."

Sunshine cocked her head. Looked from one to the other. "Maybe I've changed my mind." She moved closer to Jamie. Put a hand on his arm. "Maybe you could teach me. That might be fun."

Jamie beamed. "I'd be glad to—any time." He put his hat on his head and cocked it back.

"Are you kidding me?" Cole shook his head. "You don't have time to teach her. You've got too much work to do."

Jamie's smile faded. "But—"

"I'll teach her." Exasperation washed over him.

What was he saying? Put a weapon in the hands of that crazy vegan?

"But—"

"Go on. You've got horses waiting for you back at the ranch don't you?"

Jamie's smile flashed across his face again. "I'm going. But I'll be back. Don't let him push you around, Sunshine—his bark is worse than his bite."

IT WAS KIND of fun to tease Cole, Sunshine thought as she went back to work. She was beginning to feel like the little restaurant space could be something now that she'd scraped away the worst of the years of grime. As long as she worked within its parameters, she could turn it into a cozy space that attracted customers from all over town. She'd serve pancakes made from specialty flours in the morning for breakfast along with fruit and fresh-baked muffins and more. At lunch she'd have an array of salads, vegetable Panini's and stir-fries. For dinner she'd serve heartier fare—bean soups and vegetable stews, veggie burgers of all kinds. She'd have to fight the customers off.

She leaned against the counter and imagined the small space bustling with patrons. Intellectuals discussing the latest events. The back-to-the-earth crowd swapping tips about gardening. Hers would be the hippest spot in town.

Except... She snapped back to the present. Were there people like that in Chance Creek?

There had to be.

"Well, come on, then." Cole waved her over.

"Come on where?"

"In back. Let's start your lessons."

"Lessons? Oh—" He meant shooting lessons. "I don't think so. Not right now." No way in hell was she holding a pistol, let alone firing one.

He came closer. Everything about the man was sexy, especially when he walked. Her heartbeat speed up as he approached. "So that was all bluff back there? When Jamie was here?"

"No, I'm just busy." She turned away.

In a flash he'd moved around the counter and taken her arm.

"Hey!"

"You wanted a lesson. You're getting a lesson." He hustled her toward the door to the range. Sunshine scowled but didn't dig in her heels. When they walked into the back she took in the long galleries where targets hung at the far end. Each one was separated from the next by a thick wall. Waist-high barriers indicated where the shooter should stand. Each one was occupied.

The noise was deafening.

Shots had sounded at random all afternoon, but although still distinct out front, she'd grown used to them and had begun to shut them out of her thoughts. Now there was nothing to soften the sound.

"Here." Cole handed her a set of headphones and put some on, as well. He pressed a button on the side of her set and suddenly she could hear him more clearly. "Tap it again if you want to block out more of the noise."

They moved to stand behind Rob, who was firing at a large target decorated with the outlines of two rabbits. They looked hand-drawn. Rob quit firing, did something with his gun and laid it on the counter, hit a button on the wall, and the target traveled along a track toward them.

"Good shooting." Cole pointed to a hole outside the rabbits' outlines. "Except for that one."

"Yeah." Rob frowned. Then he took in Sunshine's presence and a smile broke over his face. "Hey, you going to take part in the contest?"

"I don't think so. Cole here just wants to show me the basics."

Cole grinned. "You should enter the contest. I'll put you up on the board and we'll get you started."

"No, I—" It was no use. Cole was determined to make a fool out of her. She turned back to Rob. "You don't know where I could find some more tables and chairs for the restaurant, do you? Cheap ones?"

"Sure I do. Want me to take you after you're done?"

That would certainly piss off Cole. "Sure. Afterward I'll buy you dinner as a thank-you."

"You don't have to do that." But he moved closer and Sunshine had a feeling he'd like a chance to spend more time with her.

He seemed nice enough. Not her type, but then who around here was?

Her gaze slid to Cole, who was returning, a target in his hand. "Mind if we take your lane, Rob?" he said.

"Not at all. I'll wait for you over here, Sunshine."

"Wait for you? What for?" Cole asked when Rob took a seat across the room.

"He's taking me shopping. And to dinner." She waited for Cole's reaction and was rewarded when he scowled.

"Stop flirting with all my customers."

"I'm not flirting. He offered." But Cole was already crossing the room. He exchanged words she couldn't hear with the cowboy and after several minutes of back and forth, Rob stood up, waved at her and left.

"What did you say to him?" She put her hands on her hips and waited for him to walk back.

"That if anyone was taking you shopping it would be me, because I know what'll fit in the space."

"We could have measured." Of all the lame excuses.

"You don't want to get mixed up with Rob. He's a real player. A woman in every port."

"I'm a big girl. I can take care of myself."

"Yeah. Let's see about that."

He led her over to the partition and talked her through the basics of firearm safety. She had to hand it to him, he was a good teacher and he made her repeat the information back several times before he moved on to allowing her to hold an unloaded pistol in her hand. She practiced identifying and moving the various parts and gripping it correctly. Only then did he load it with cartridges and walk her through firing her first shot.

When she pulled the trigger for the first time she gasped as the shot fired. She'd thought she might be scared, but instead she felt… invigorated.

"Can I do it again?" she asked, turning toward him.

"Whoa! Whoa there!" He stopped her and she quickly remembered she had to keep the muzzle pointed down the shooting lane.

"Sorry!"

"You bet your ass you're sorry. Anyone who forgets that rule finds himself on the street."

"Okay, I got it."

He waited until she was back in the correct stance. "Beginner's mistake. Take a deep breath and try again."

She did. And again and again, gaining confidence as she went. She couldn't believe she was hitting the target—even though her shots were nowhere near the round bulls-eye on the paper. When Cole declared her lesson over and packed the pistol away, Sunshine turned around to find she had quite an audience. The men clapped and she blushed, then made a little curtsy, deciding to enjoy the moment. When her gaze found Cole's, he was smiling, too. "You did all right."

"Thanks."

"See?" Rob had slipped back into the gallery at some point when her back was turned. "It's pretty cool, right?"

"I guess so."

"I thought I told you to skedaddle," Cole said to him.

"Come on, Sunshine. Let's go do that shopping," Rob said.

"OUT!"

Rob laughed and pretended to cower at Cole's angry outburst. "Another time," he whispered to her, squeezing her hand and left again.

"I'll be ready in five minutes," she told Cole, handing him the headphones.

"Ready for what?"

"Shopping!" Why else had he shooed Rob away again? "I hope you know where I can find enough tables within my budget."

Chapter Seven

WHY WAS HE shopping when he was supposed to be running his business? Not that the range couldn't run itself half the time. All his customers knew what they owed him and how to work the old cash register. They knew where the extra targets were, too.

Still.

"Here we are." He pulled into a gravel parking lot.

Sunshine eyed the second-hand store doubtfully. Kerri's Collectibles was a hodge-podge of used goods, but more than once Cole had found something he needed inside. Plus he'd much rather give a hometown girl like Kerri Olsen the business than some big box store in Billings. He led Sunshine inside and ushered her toward the furniture section.

Sunshine made a beeline for a square pedestal table that had been painted blue at some point in the past. "This one looks good."

"Really?" He tried again. "I mean… sure."

"I'd get this old paint off, of course. Refinish it."

Cole looked at her in surprise. "You know how to do that?"

"Sure." She'd moved on to another circular table. Testing it out, she discovered it wobbled and made a face. "I don't know about this one. I guess I could jam something underneath it."

"I could fix it." Cole sighed inwardly at his own stupidity. Why on earth would he volunteer to do that? She had to lose. He might decide at some point to pursue this exasperatingly beautiful woman, but it would be after he'd secured the building for himself.

"That's terrific. I guess I'll take it after all. Let's see what else they have."

"Can I help you with anything?"

"Hi, Kerri." Cole smiled at the woman who'd come to meet them. Kerri Olsen had taken over the shop from her grandmother a couple of years ago and the job seemed to suit her. Cole remembered her hanging on the fringes when they were in school. Artistic and sensitive, she hadn't really fit in. As an adult she'd found her niche with the second-hand store. She had a way of finding objects that deserved a second life and displaying them imaginatively.

"Sunshine here is looking for tables."

"I want these two." Sunshine pointed out the ones she'd already claimed. "I need some more, though. I'm starting a restaurant."

She said this last part rather shyly and to Cole's surprise, he wanted to step closer to her and protect her from any harsh response. Which was crazy. Kerri was the last person to respond harshly to anyone's dreams.

"That's terrific! Do you have a location in mind?"

Sunshine flushed and Cole chuckled. "Right in the front room of my rifle range."

"Oh. Well." Kerri didn't seem to know how to respond to that.

"It's a strange situation," Sunshine said.

"Life is full of strange situations. Here, what about this one?" Kerri led the way around a cluster of couches to a rather battered small table that currently served to hold up a lamp. "You'll want some two-people tables and some bigger ones, right?"

"That's right." Sunshine frowned. "I guess I should have drawn up a plan first. I was just too excited to get started."

"Do you know the dimensions of the room?" Both women turned to Cole and once again he wondered how he'd ended up helping Sunshine when she was trying to take away his business.

"Roughly thirty by thirty."

Kerri pulled out her phone and punched some numbers in. "With some space taken up by walkways and so on, I'd say you could seat about forty people. So maybe seven tables of four and six tables for two? Or maybe you'll want one big table for larger parties?" She indicated a table Cole hadn't even noticed—a long trestle-style rectangle.

Sunshine brightened. "I like that. I want larger parties to feel welcome."

"What kind of food will you serve?" Together they went to examine the table. Cole braced himself for Kerri's reaction to Sunshine's answer.

"Vegan cuisine."

To her credit, Kerri only wavered for a minute. "Vegan? That's like, no meat or dairy?"

"That's right."

"Wow. That's… interesting. Can I ask what made you choose a shooting range to put a vegan restaurant? That seems like two very different crowds."

Once again, Cole was impressed with Kerri's diplomacy. "Very different," he put in.

"I didn't have a lot of choice," Sunshine said after a moment's hesitation. "I hope that when people get a chance to taste my cooking they'll change their minds about vegan food."

"I'm sure they will." But Kerri sent Cole a look over Sunshine's head when she turned away to examine the table. Cole shrugged. It wasn't his business if Sunshine's restaurant flopped. In fact, he hoped it did.

Although…

He hated to admit it but he felt bad about how Sunshine would react when she inevitably did fail. He had the feeling Sunshine would be crushed.

Not your problem, he told himself. *You've got your own business to run and two dozen tenants depending on you to do it well.*

Somehow that didn't make him feel any better.

"DO YOU NEED any help refurbishing the tables?" Kerri asked as she helped carry them out to the parking lot.

"Maybe. Do you like that kind of thing?" Sunshine set her end of the table down near Cole's truck. Cole was on the phone to Rob and Jamie to see if they'd come help transport all the tables back to the range.

"Are you kidding? I love it!"

"Me, too." They grinned at each other. "I'll be working on them all day tomorrow so stop by the rifle range any time."

"Where are you living?"

Heat suffused Sunshine's face. "I... uh... I'm sharing the apartment behind the range."

"With Cole?" Kerri's eyebrows shot up. "Are you and Cole an item?"

"No. Not at all. We're just... it's complicated."

Kerri grinned. "I'll bet. Everything's complicated until you take your clothes off."

"Shh!" Sunshine cast a look over her shoulder to make sure Cold hadn't heard.

The other woman giggled. "Come on, don't tell me you haven't done it. Or at least thought about it, for heaven's sake. Cole's one of the hottest guys in town."

"There are plenty of handsome men in town."

"Is there someone else you've met that you like?"

Cole ended his call and came to stand next to her, his expression inscrutable. "Rob will be here in a few minutes," he said.

"Thanks."

When Cole moved away again, Kerri leaned closer. "Is it Rob? Rob Matheson? He's cute, too."

Cole didn't say a word, but his shoulders stiffened and Sunshine groaned inwardly. She didn't have the slightest crush on Rob Matheson. She didn't have a crush on anyone.

Certainly not on the hottest guy in town.

Chapter Eight

ROB MATHESON? SUNSHINE had a crush on Rob? Cole's fingers tightened into fists. When had she even had time to form an opinion about the man? If she liked anyone it should be—

He broke that thought off and paced away. It didn't matter who Sunshine liked or what she did. Soon enough she'd be gone.

Irritation suffused him as he remembered how he'd thought Cecily might be trying to throw him and Sunshine together. That was a laugh. Sunshine wouldn't stop until she'd driven him out of the building. And if he was the one to prevail she'd hate his guts and leave. Then he'd be stuck with all these stupid tables. He'd have to set up a poker tournament to make use of them.

Now, that wasn't such a bad idea, he mused. He could see a group of Chance Creek's men getting together on Wednesday nights for a game or two. It would be a way to earn some extra money. If Sunshine would serve ribs and burgers instead of chicken scratch and Melba toast, those men would probably make a night of it.

By the time Rob's truck pulled into the parking lot and he climbed out, Cole had forgotten he was supposed to be mad at him.

"Hi, Sunshine. Hi, Kerri." Rob tipped his hat at both of them and got to work, and while he was flirtatious, he didn't seem to favor one of the women over the other. Cole's temper was soothed and soon enough they'd driven the short distance to the range and unloaded all the tables and chairs into the front space.

"See you all tomorrow," Rob said when they were through. Cole thought that would be the end of him for the night but he hesitated on his way to the front door. "Sunshine? I know you don't know many people in town yet. Any chance you want to go to dinner with me tonight?"

Sunshine smiled and all Cole's anger came rushing back. He was only mad because the men who were supposed to be his friends were cozying up to his enemy, he told himself. But that was a lie. The truth was, the thought of Rob, or any of them, touching Sunshine made him want to lose his mind.

"I'm taking her out to dinner tonight. Bug off!" he said.

Sunshine spun around to look at him. "But—"

"We'll see you tomorrow, Rob. Good-bye." Cole shoved the man bodily out the door. Sunshine was staring at him when he came back in.

"That wasn't necessary."

"That was necessary. Rob's a good guy. I don't want you leading him on. You won't be staying here long enough to be anyone's girlfriend."

She rolled her eyes at him and headed toward the front door. "I thought you said he was a player."

"Where are you going?"

"To the store to get myself something to cook for dinner."

"The hell with that. I said I'm taking you out, so I'm taking you out." He grabbed her hand, wrapping his fingers tightly around hers. "Come on."

"YOU MUST BE new in town," the hostess said as she led them to a table in the middle of the bustling diner. "And you've already caught the eye of the most eligible bachelor around. Lucky you."

"Come on, now, Tracey. I'm hardly that eligible." Cole winked at the young woman and Sunshine felt a stab of emotion she couldn't identify. Surely it wasn't jealousy.

"You're cute as a button. That's all I require." Tracey winked back and strode away to greet her next customers.

"Cute as a button?" Sunshine repeated. To her delight, Cole reddened.

"I've known Tracey forever. She lives in one of the apartment buildings out back."

"Is some kind of a cowgirl posse going to ambush me now that I've caught the eye of the most *eligible bachelor in town*?"

Cole didn't say anything, but his glance flicked over her in a way that let her know that she had caught *his* eye. At least a little. Now her face felt warm. "What's good to eat here?"

"Good luck on finding anything vegan."

"I can always find something vegan."

She did this time too, although it took some work. She ended up with a salad, minus the dairy-rich house dressing, and some garlic toast made especially with margarine rather than butter.

"I don't think I've ever had someone request margarine before," Tracey said when Sunshine ordered. But she wrote down her request, and Sunshine's careful taste test of her food when she received it told her the kitchen had honored it.

"You take the cake," Cole told her, biting into a thick piece of meatloaf.

"Why?"

He chewed and swallowed. "Little thing like you giving out orders left and right. 'Move my furniture, deliver my tables, give me margarine instead of butter.'" He chirped his recital.

"I don't give orders. I make requests."

"Yeah, yeah." But he was looking at her as if he was somewhat proud of her determination. How strange was that?

"It's busy here."

"People like diner food."

"You think I'm going to fail, don't you?"

He put his fork and knife down. "Here's the thing, Sunshine. I know you're going to fail. That should make me happy. But it's kind of like watching a puppy face off with a steamroller. You've got to feel bad for the dog."

"Are you calling me a dog?" She glared at him. "Or is that your roundabout way of saying I'm a bitch?"

A few people from surrounding tables looked their way. Cole leaned forward. "I didn't say anything like that. I called you a puppy. Puppies are cute."

"And stupid."

"Inexperienced," he countered.

"You really don't think I know anything about running a restaurant?"

"Well, do you?"

"Yes." She toyed with her fork as she remembered the disaster back in Chicago. It wasn't the food or the location or her inexperience or anything she'd done that had made it end so badly, though. That was all Greg's fault. He'd broken her heart.

"Didn't go well, did it?"

"It's not what you think."

He leaned back. "Oh, yeah? What was it then? Too much tofu?"

"Too much cheating." She shut her eyes, wishing she could take those words back.

"Someone was pilfering money?" Cole straightened up.

She shook her head. "It doesn't matter."

He narrowed his eyes. "You mean someone cheated on you. A boyfriend?"

He obviously wasn't going to give up until he knew the story. "I invested in my boyfriend's restaurant. I gave him all my money. I thought we were partners and that we'd build the place together and for a while it was like that. We were talking about marriage and kids and..." She trailed off. "I found him with another woman."

"I'm sorry." Cole sat back in the booth. He did seem sorry. "Tough break."

"Yeah." She pushed the heartache and humiliation that still burned inside her away. "It was a tough break. Now I'm moving on. Alone."

Chapter Nine

WHEN HE UNLOCKED the door to the apartment, giving the heavy panel a shove with his shoulder, Cole thought about the things he'd learned at dinner time. No wonder Sunshine had such a chip on her shoulder when it came to men—and to sharing the range building. She'd been screwed over before—and the truth was she would be screwed over again when he won and reasserted his right to the premises.

He couldn't allow himself to care about her feelings, though. Not in this instance. In order to preserve his own income and keep his tenants off the street, he had to win this contest.

Sunshine trailed inside after him and went to perch on the sofa. He realized she couldn't go to bed until he'd cleared out of the main room, so he said goodnight, used the bathroom and retired to his room.

He could hear her moving around the apartment, getting ready for bed herself. It took all the strength of will he had not to picture her undressing and sliding between the covers on his couch. He thought he'd struggle to fall asleep but he must have dozed off fairly quickly because when he woke again, the clock read half-past three in the morning.

He'd heard something—something which registered as not belonging to the normal sounds in the apartment at night. He didn't want to scare Sunshine, or make her think he was spying on her, but he had to check it out. Easing out of bed, he slid his boxer briefs on, crossed the room, opened the door a crack and peered out. Sunshine was sitting at the dining room table, a pad of paper in front of her and a pen in her hand. The overhead light was on but the rest of the apartment was dark. Relief coursing through him, he pushed the door the rest of the way open and walked toward her.

"Can't sleep?"

Sunshine started, then caught herself and nodded. "I'm revising my menu."

He came to stand by the table, noticed Sunshine wouldn't meet his eyes and realized his lack of clothing was disconcerting her.

Or maybe it was the lack of her own. She wore another barely there nightgown that was appropriate for the Montana heat, but not appropriate for a middle-of-the-night conversation with an almost stranger.

Still, he appreciated it.

When Sunshine raised her gaze and caught him appreciating it, he grinned. "Are you adding steak?"

"Steak?"

"To your menu. That's what will pull in the customers around here."

"No. I'm not adding steak." She tapped her pen on

the paper. "I will add chili and at least one stew, though. Vegan chili and stew."

"Sounds delightful."

He thought she would scowl at him but instead the corner of her mouth quirked up. "It is delightful. I'm a terrific cook."

"Know what? I bet you are. But you're a lousy businesswoman. You don't get rich by deciding what customers want. You get rich by asking them what they want and giving it to them."

"Says the man with the failing rifle range."

"It's not failing."

"Really? Then why not take it somewhere else?"

"Because..." Because she was right; after paying his mortgage he barely made enough to pay the bills. "Because it's always been right here. I'm honoring my father's memory." And keeping Tracey, Scott and William off the street.

"People will like the food I make." She didn't sound entirely sure, though. Cole expected that now that she'd met his customers she was forming a new idea of the clientele she might expect.

"Suit yourself." He shrugged. "The sooner you shut down and leave, the better for me. Goodnight."

But he didn't leave. In fact, he didn't know what came over him as he rounded the corner of the table and dropped a kiss on top of Sunshine's head.

And as he strode back to his room and shut the door behind him, he had no idea why she let him.

Chapter Ten

SUNSHINE WASN'T SURE how Aunt Cecily had managed it, but when she went to get the paperwork and inspections for the restaurant, it turned out she'd somehow greased the skids, and everything went more smoothly and quickly than she'd dreamed possible. Now three weeks later she was ready for opening day—as ready as she could get.

The local paper had done a write-up of her new venture—and of Cole's rifle range—and she hoped that translated into hordes of patrons coming to try out her food. She'd prepared a couple of dishes for the reporter to try, which the reporter did, after a lot of coaxing. He'd seemed pleasantly surprised, although he'd written up her chili as a bit bland. She'd come up with a new, spicier mix, and on a whim added a full-bodied beer to the recipe to give it more heft. Plus, she had a feeling that adding that beer's name to the description of the dish might just draw in a few meat and potatoes types who otherwise wouldn't be impressed.

At eight in the morning, she decided to call Kate for a last-minute pep talk. They'd only spoken a couple of times in the past few weeks, once when Kate let her know there was no clear way to challenge Cecily's will, and again one night when Kate's date was late picking her up. Both times Sunshine felt their conversation was stiff and awkward, mostly because she kept remembering Kate thought she was a drama queen, but she decided to give it another try. They'd been friends for years, and just because she'd left Chicago, that shouldn't change, even if Kate's characterization of her did sting. She grabbed her phone and headed for the back deck for privacy, only remembering as she shut the door behind her that Kate wasn't all that receptive to talking about her problems anymore.

Was she being dramatic this time, calling for help to boost her spirits? Sunshine didn't think so. She dialed Kate's number before she could second-guess herself.

"Hi," she said as cheerfully as possible when Kate answered. "It's been ages since we chatted. How are you?"

"It hasn't been that long." Kate was obviously at work, and Sunshine's resolve began to fade.

"My restaurant opens today. I just wanted to let you know."

"That's terrific. How do you think you'll do? Did you run a splashy advertising campaign?"

Sunshine's spirits sunk further. Kate knew she had no money for ad campaigns. "I did what I could."

"I'm sure that'll be fine."

She held back a sigh at Kate's lack of interest. "You sound distracted. I better let you go." In the old days,

Kate would have been all apologies and they'd end up talking for the better part of a half-hour, work or no work. Not today, though.

"I do need to go. All this dating has made it impossible to work nights, which means I'm behind all the time."

"Of course. I'm glad you're having fun."

"You know what? For the first time in ages, I am having fun." Kate's voice took on a dreamy tone and Sunshine felt a stab of jealousy. "I guess I'm not being a very good friend, though, am I?" Kate suddenly added. "I know you're used to a lot more of my time. I really am sorry."

"It's really okay." It was, Sunshine decided as they said their good-byes and hung up. Kate needed the balance of love in her life or she'd work all the time. She wasn't responsible for Sunshine's happiness.

That was her own job and Sunshine decided from now on she would handle it herself. She was starting a business, making a new life for herself, showing the world she could stand on her own two feet. She didn't need Kate or anyone else to prop her up.

That didn't make her feel any less lonely, however.

Sunshine decided to throw herself into her work. This was first-day jitters, nothing more. As soon as things got started and she was busy, she wouldn't miss Kate at all. The range opened at ten in the morning and she planned to open her restaurant right along with it today. She left the apartment and let herself into the front of the building. Cole was in the range, doing whatever it was he did to prepare for his days. She decided to give the tables a final polish.

They'd fallen into a kind of armed truce over the past few weeks. They kept to their portions of the business and circled around each other warily when they were at home. There'd been no more late-night trysts in their undergarments, for which Sunshine told herself she was grateful, but which left her somehow disappointed. Every day Ethan, Jamie, Rob and Cab made their appearances to try to improve their scores for the contest. Every day they made various plays for her attention, which was kind of fun. And every day Cole chased them out again.

But he didn't flirt with her in their place.

Why did she wish he would?

The front door swung open at five minutes to ten and Kerri strode through. She, too, had become a regular. Sunshine had grown to look forward to her visits. She was funny, practical and artistic all in one, and she'd been a great help with the décor of the café. She wasn't Kate, but she was proving herself to be a good friend.

"All set for the big day? Yum—it smells great in here."

"Thanks." Sunshine indicated all the empty tables. "Take your pick. I'll bring you a menu."

"Don't mind if I do."

"I'll give you a minute," Sunshine said when she handed the menu to Kerri. The door swung open again and Jamie walked in. Cole emerged from the range and lingered by his counter.

"You must be ready to work on your scores."

"In a bit," Jamie said. "First I want some lunch."

"At ten in the morning?"

"I've been up since four."

Cole frowned.

Jamie spotted Kerri. "Darn it," he said, pulling a huge bouquet of flowers out from behind his back. "I wanted to be Sunshine's first customer. I guess you had the same idea."

"That's right," Kerri said, "but I didn't think to bring flowers."

Jamie offered them to Sunshine and chose a table near Kerri's while she went off to find a vase. A minute later Ethan arrived and joined him. Sunshine fetched them both menus. Happiness swooped through her; she was doing it. She had opened her own restaurant and two minutes before her official open time, two tables were occupied. She squashed the fear that these would be her only customers.

She busied herself behind the counter for a minute, filling glasses of water for everyone to give them time to make up their minds about what to order. When Cab and Rob came in and headed straight for Ethan and Jamie's table, she beamed at Cole triumphantly.

Kerri was smiling and humming to herself, reading over the menu with interest. The men seemed to be in close consultation and another pang of fear zipped through Sunshine. Was she making a colossal fool out of herself by trying to interest her customers in vegan fare? Was Cole right—was she going to crash and burn? She engaged in deep breathing exercises until she had the sense that everyone was ready to order. Then she brought her tray of water glasses around, gave one to each of them, and pulled out a pad of paper.

"What can I get you?" She started with Kerri, hoping the woman would lead the way boldly, and the men would fall in line behind her.

"I'll try the mock taco wraps." Kerri smiled. "They sound great."

Sunshine scribbled a note on the pad. "How about you, Jamie? What'll it be?"

The cowboy scanned the menu again. "I guess I'll try the burger, although I don't get how you can have a burger without beef."

"You'll be pleasantly surprised," Sunshine assured him.

"At the very least you'll be surprised."

Sunshine whipped around when Cole spoke. Was he going to heckle her? That wasn't fair.

"It's really good," Sunshine said. "Rob? How about you?"

"Bring me the biggest bowl of chili you got and a slice of cornbread about this wide." He held up his hands to demonstrate and smiled. Sunshine had been on the receiving end of that smile many times. She had to hand it to Rob—he was cute. So were all of them for that matter. Still, it was only Cole who set her heart beating fast. It figured.

"Will do."

"You can't go wrong with chili," Rob explained to the others, dampening her good will toward him a little.

Cole snorted. "When chili goes wrong, though, it really goes wrong."

Sunshine ignored him.

"I'll have the Linguine Alfredo," Cab said.

"Would you like to order a side of vegetables?"

Before she could list them, the big man shook his head. "Vegetables and me keep our distance for the most part," he confessed.

She bit back a laugh at his sheepish grin. "I'll have you eating lots of vegetables before I'm done with you."

"Good luck with that," Cole called over. "Cab wouldn't know a cauliflower if it bit him on the butt."

The sheriff turned slowly around in his chair and fixed Cole with a look. "*I'm* not the ignoramus in the room." He turned back to Sunshine. "Honey, you cook me up any vegetable you like. I'll eat every last bit."

A glance told her Cole was seething. He was shuffling papers around his counter, his jaw hard. She touched Cab's arm. "Thank you, Sheriff. You won't regret it."

"I'll take the pizza," Ethan said, handing her his menu. "Even if there ain't any meat on it."

"Perfect. I'll be back with your orders as soon as I can."

She had only gone three steps when chaos erupted behind her.

"Hey!" Jamie leaped to his feet. "Damn it, Cole—that's not fair!"

"For God's sake!"

"Cole, stop it!"

She turned to see Cole scrubbing furiously at the whiteboard he'd placed on the wall, erasing the men's scores one by one and replacing them with new ones that were substantially lower.

"From now on, anyone who eats at Sunshine's gets ten points off. Per meal."

"That's low, even for you," Sunshine declared, putting her hands on her hips. "Are you afraid you can't win any other way?"

Cole closed the gap between them and towered over her. "I can win any way we play it. I'm just making something clear." He straightened. Turned on his friends. "You're either with me or against me."

He strode to the range door and shut it hard behind him.

"Well, hell," Jamie said. "Don't that take the cake."

Sunshine resumed her walk toward the counter, fury building within her at every step. He was going to do everything he could to undercut her, wasn't he? Whether or not it was fair. She'd have to think of a few tricks of her own.

Her hands were shaking as she prepared the meals, but more deep breaths helped keep her panic at bay. Most of the preparation was simple—the chili was bubbling on the stove already, and she'd done as much prep work on all her offerings as she possibly could. Less than fifteen minutes later, she was able to serve all the meals.

"It looks great," Cab said loudly.

"Yum." Ethan surveyed his pizza with interest, although when he spied a piece of artichoke heart he squinted at it as if unsure what it was.

As usual, Kerri was the most enthusiastic. "I know I'm going to love it."

Sunshine resisted the urge to hover while everyone took their first bites, but she didn't go far either, making the rounds of the room and straightening up tables and chairs that were already straight. If she wasn't careful, Cole was going to ruin her business before it had a chance to flourish. The men might eat here today, but after what he'd done, they'd be afraid to come back. She had to convince them Cole couldn't hurt them.

Then it hit her—she'd fight fire with fire. Slipping back behind the counter, she pulled out a pack of printer paper which she'd been using to make lists and jot down recipe ideas since the day she moved in. She pulled out a roll of tape, too, and began to tape sheets of paper together end to end. When she'd created a banner large enough to satisfy her, she used a black marker to write, "Sunshine's Scones and Six Packs!" Underneath that headline, she made a chart similar to the one Cole had made on his whiteboards. Instead of shooting categories, however, she made her own ten events. She labeled one *Compliments*. She labeled another one *Adventurousness*. She labeled a third *Vegetables* and a fourth *Clean Your Plate*. When she was done, she carried the whole awkward quilt of paper squares over to her own side wall and tacked it up under the high windows.

"What's that?" Jamie called out.

"It's my own contest. You can get points, just like in Cole's." She demonstrated, pointing out the categories. "If you say something nice about your meal, you get a point." She used the marker to jot down each of their names and gave them each a point. "Every time you try a new entrée you get a point." She gave them each another point. "Every time you try a new vegetable side dish you get a point." Cab got a point, which made the sheriff grin. "Every time you clean your plate you get a point. The winner with the most points at the end of the contest gets a six pack every week for a year." She shoved the cap on the pen in triumph.

"Beer? For real? I thought you were vegan." Rob leaned forward.

"Beer is vegan."

"Hot damn," Jamie said. "This vegan stuff ain't so bad."

Chapter Eleven

COLE TOOK A steadying breath and let it out slowly while firing the Glock 30 at a target his previous rounds had already torn practically to shreds. Ammunition was expensive, and he was going through it like a house on fire, but when he'd seen his friends in Sunshine's café, something had gone off inside him until he lost his cool. Didn't they know what they were doing to him? Did they want him to lose?

He stopped firing when he ran out of rounds and automatically went through the precautions that had been drilled into him since childhood. Put on the safety, check the action, place the pistol on the counter before turning around. He was the only one in the range, though. Everyone else was helping Sunshine steal his future right out from under him.

If they didn't come to shoot afterward it would be his own damn fault, too. Yelling at her like that—and at them, too.

For the first time he considered what he'd do if he lost the range. He couldn't open a new one and what else was he good for except running a business? He thought of the tenants in the apartment buildings. What would they do? Would they find homes elsewhere or would it be the final blow to some of them that left them truly homeless?

Thirty minutes later, he couldn't stand anymore to be alone with his thoughts. He opened the door to the front room and found his friends still lolling in the chairs around Sunshine's mismatched tables. Several of them seemed to be on their second meals.

"Cole—you gotta try this pizza!" Ethan said.

"Pizza with fake cheese? I don't think so."

Ethan pulled the slice he was about to bite into away from his mouth. "Fake cheese?" He looked to Sunshine for confirmation.

"It's not fake—it's just not made from cow's milk."

"Sounds pretty fake to me." Cole came out from behind his counter and approached the table. "How much other fake food have you served my friends?"

"None of it is fake." Sunshine came out from behind her counter too. "It's alternative."

"An alternative to eating real food." He spotted Jamie's plate. "What the hell is that?"

"Zucchini. It's a vegetable."

"I know it's a vegetable." Was he even having this conversation? The closest thing to a vegetable he could ever remember seeing Jamie eat was the French fries at the Burger Shack.

"I've got artichokes on my pizza." Ethan held one out.

"My cauliflower ain't half bad, either. Sunshine did

something lemony to it."

She'd gotten the sheriff to eat a vegetable? Cole's anger was building again. He knew why all his friends were following her lead like puppies; that slinky outfit she was prancing around in had mesmerized them. Every curve of hers was on display and all that long, blond hair. It was enough to drive a man wild.

His gaze landed on a makeshift banner she'd hung on the wall. "What's that?"

"It's my Scones and Six Packs contest."

His fingers bunched into fists. No way. She wouldn't.

"It's awesome. All you have to do is eat things to rack up points," Rob said, polishing off the last of what looked to be some kind of rice dish.

"Let me guess; the grand prize is a six pack every week of the year."

"You got it," Sunshine said sweetly.

"You can't do that."

"Why not? It's a free country."

"It's not a free rifle range!"

"The rifle range starts over there." Sunshine pointed to his makeshift counter and the door behind it. "Over here it's my café and my café is definitely free."

"Oh yeah?" He'd taken just about all he could handle. First she'd hijacked his business, then she hijacked his friends and now she wanted to hijack his contest? He strode to the counter, grabbed a muffin from a pile she must have just lifted from a baking tin and hurled it across the room.

Cab had pushed his chair back when Cole started shouting, and he stood up just in time for the muffin to peg him in the forehead. He didn't flinch. He brushed the crumbs from his shirt, peered down at its remains on the floor and carefully stepped past them.

"We got a problem here?"

"Yeah, we've got a problem." Anger overcame Cole's common sense. Two steps brought him to Sunshine's banner. He jabbed a finger at it. "Why the hell do I see your name listed here, Cab? What did I tell you about eating in her restaurant?"

Cab crossed his arms. "You're telling me where I can and can't eat?"

"Better stay in my café, Cab," Sunshine said. "Cole's running a dictatorship over there." She waved a hand toward the other side of the room.

"I'm not running a dictatorship. I'm running a business," Cole exploded. "A business that's going to go out of business if you keep this up." He jabbed the banner again. "But maybe you all don't care. Maybe you've got another indoor range to shoot at. Maybe an indoor range is a stupid, God-damned waste of time!"

He had never been one for dramatic exits before, but he crossed the room before anyone could answer him and slammed the front door shut behind him.

There was no sense staying at a business that had no customers. No sense watching Sunshine make a mockery of everything he'd built. He'd go home where he could be by himself.

But when he entered the apartment there were signs

of Sunshine everywhere. He sagged against the door and gave in to the awareness that had been growing ever since she arrived.

He wasn't going to win.

"WELL, HECK," ETHAN said. "Didn't mean to make Cole so mad."

"He backed himself into that corner," Rob said.

"But it's true, ain't it?" Jamie said. "If Sunshine wins, Cole loses."

"And if Cole wins, Sunshine loses," Ethan pointed out. "No offense, Sunshine, but your Aunt Cecily had a mean streak, didn't she?"

Sunshine sighed as she got the broom and began to sweep up the muffin bits. "You know, I haven't been able to figure that out. She was always so nice to me. Sounds like she was nice to Cole, too. I think she made too many promises to both of us, and didn't know what to do in the end."

"Maybe she expected you to figure out how to do things fairly between yourselves," Cab said, sitting back down again.

"How? I'd buy Cole's half of the business if I could, but I don't have any money for that."

"I don't know where else Cole would put an indoor range, anyhow," Jamie said. "It takes a pretty special building."

"It would be easier to move the café," Ethan said.

Sunshine blinked. She shouldn't expect Cole's friends to take her side, but somehow she hadn't expected them to give her the boot, either.

"No one's saying you have to move," Cab told her. "Just that it might be easier."

"Cole doesn't have the money to buy me out, though," she said. "Doesn't matter," she added bitterly, her former excitement and happiness about opening day suddenly disappearing like a puff of smoke in the wind. "Look around you. You're my only customers. I'm going to lose anyhow."

"You won't lose," Kerri said loyally. "You need more advertising, though. No one knows you're here. Let me whip up a brochure for you this afternoon and you can start delivering them to people tonight. Laundromats, gas stations, places like that."

"You'd do that for me?"

"Of course I would. But the guys are right; maybe you and Cole need to think of another way to sort this out."

"Time for me to get back to work," Cab said. "Hang in there, Sunshine."

Chapter Twelve

C OLE WAS SEATED at the dining room table, beer in hand, when the door opened much later that night and Sunshine let herself in. She came to a halt when she spotted him there.

"Go ahead and yell," she said tiredly. "But there's not much to be angry about. I only had two more customers after your friends went home."

An unexpected jolt of pity shot through him. He'd been angry for the first few hours, but he'd had plenty of time to simmer down over the course of the afternoon and evening. Was he really angry at Sunshine? Or was he angry at himself for not having saved anything for a rainy day and not having much in the way of future prospects, either? Angry because he hadn't paid enough attention in the early days and stopped his father from sucking every last dime out of the business? Angry because far too many people depended on him to make this work?

"Business can be slow."

She nodded, walked by him into the kitchen where he heard the sink running and returned with a glass of water. She set it on the table by him and went to fetch her laptop.

"Checking your e-mail?"

"Coming up with a new plan," she said. "I was so worried about having the menu and tables and chairs ready, I didn't plan a marketing campaign. It's time for me to start."

"What do you have in mind?" Cole was proficient with a computer, but he wasn't exactly adventurous with it.

"I'll start with social media. I'll post fun images of my food, my daily specials, coupons, things like that. Maybe I'll put my Scones and Six Packs contest online, too." She shot him a look as she sat down.

"Great."

"I can't find the rifle range online," she said a moment later.

"I've never gotten around to it."

"You should at least have a website with your hours on it—things like that."

"Never learned how."

"Huh." She bent over her computer, typed furiously for a bit, then bit her lip and frowned, as if hunting for something. Whatever it was, she found it and got busy again. Just when Cole thought she was letting him know she was done talking for the night, she turned the laptop around. "There. What do you think?"

Surprise washed over him at the sight of the website she'd just whipped up. It was plain—just the name of his business with an image of a rifle range that kind of resembled his. It listed his business hours—Sunshine must have memorized them—and some of the services he offered. He squinted. "And an on-site café?"

"An on-site café is a terrific sales point." She grinned at him.

"An on-site vegan café isn't quite as much." But when her grin faded away he felt a pang of regret. "Seems like the guys liked your food," he added.

"I think they thought it was all right," she said thoughtfully. "But they would prefer burgers and steaks."

"They would."

Her shoulders slumped. "I need to get the word out to the vegan crowd that I'm here."

"Or you need to change your menu."

"That's like me saying you should offer dance classes in the range."

He thought about that. "Okay, scratch that. You need to make your vegan food more manly."

"Manly vegan food." She tapped her finger on the table. "That's a great name for a cookbook. Speaking of which, have you ever considered making videos?"

"I'm not sure I follow that transition." Sunshine was awfully cute working away at her computer. Alone with her he was all too aware of her curves. If only they weren't mortal enemies, she'd make a terrific girlfriend. He stood up and moved to her side of the table. Sat down in the chair beside her.

"Well, you know a lot about guns, right?" she said.

"Firearms? Sure I do."

"What if you made videos about various things and established yourself as kind of an expert?"

"I don't know about being an expert."

She fixed him with a look. "Here's the big secret, Cole. No one is really an expert. You just decide to be one and hustle until you can convince everyone else. If you posted a video each week and used social media consistently, you might just build up a following. People would know about you and your range. They'd drive farther to come see it and shoot here." She smiled saucily. "And I'd get more customers for my café."

"I see. It's all a dirty trick to steal my building." He elbowed her playfully.

"It's my building." She elbowed him back.

He leaned against her elbow, impervious to her pokes, and stole a kiss.

"Hey!" She pulled back and Cole cursed. Sunshine lifted her hand to her mouth. "What was that for?"

"For being so damn sexy all the time."

Her eyes went wide. "I'm not a bit sexy!" He raised his eyebrows and to his amusement, she actually blushed. "I don't try to be."

"Some women don't have to try. They just are. You're one of them."

His praise seemed to fluster her all the more. Cole figured he'd just found Sunshine's Achilles heel. "That body of yours just keeps on going, doesn't it?"

"I don't even know what that means."

Cole wasn't sure he did, either, but it sounded dirty and she was practically climbing out of her seat with embarrassment. "If you took off your clothes, you'd stop traffic."

She rolled her eyes. "Anyone nude stops traffic."

"But you nude would be heaven on earth." He stumbled to a stop, heat warming his own cheeks. He'd given himself away there, hadn't he?

Sunshine straightened. "You're trying to get me into bed."

"No, I'm not." He moved back.

"Yes, you are. You think if I sleep with you I'll stop competing with you. You think you're so hot that I'll let you win."

"Well, am I? Hot enough that making love to me would turn your head every which way around?" He bent forward again.

"You're not even remotely hot," she scoffed.

Ouch. But wait a minute, Sunshine didn't seem to be able to meet his eyes. Maybe he was remotely hot, after all. He reached back and pulled his T-shirt over his head.

"What are you doing?"

"Giving you a better look." He stood up. Flexed his bicep and stuck it close to her. Sunshine cringed back. "Feel that."

"I'm not feeling that."

"Scaredy-cat. You're afraid that if you touch my muscles you'll get so turned on you'll jump me."

"Fat chance."

"Prove it."

Sunshine was getting angry. She tapped a finger on

his bicep. "There? Satisfied?"

"Not hardly." Cole didn't know what had taken possession of him, but he'd tried everything else and all it got him was failure. He was determined to succeed at this. He lifted Sunshine bodily out of her seat. "Pretty strong, huh?"

"Put me down." He set her on her feet and she glared at him. "You're acting like a caveman."

"You're acting like a coward."

"How can you say that?"

"Because you won't touch me, that's how." He made the muscle again. "Go on."

With a theatrical sigh, Sunshine lay her hand on his bicep. A wicked smile curved her lips suddenly as she began to pet it. Then she bent close and before he could pull away, she rubbed her cheek against his bicep like a cat.

"See? Still not jumping your bones." She smiled triumphantly and turned away.

Her cheek against his skin had made every nerve stand on end, even though he knew she was teasing him. He reached out, spun her around and pulled her into a kiss.

A real kiss. The kind of kiss he'd been aching to steal since the night she moved in. Sunshine went rigid in his arms, but just when he thought he'd made a big mistake, she sighed and leaned into him. Cole's entire body went on alert. He couldn't help himself. He wrapped his arms around her and kissed Sunshine the way God meant for men to kiss women.

When he came up for air some time later, Sunshine was breathing heavily. And shaking her head.

"We can't do this."

"Why not?" He was ready to do it again.

"Because we're enemies."

"We don't have to be." He was holding onto her, his palms cupping her elbows. He slid his hands up her arms and drew her even closer. "I can think of better things for us to be."

"Like what?" Her voice was barely a whisper.

"Like the kind of people who sleep together."

She stiffened again. Pushed him away. "I don't think so."

He came after her. "Come on, Sunshine. You want it as much as I do."

She shook her head. All the warmth had gone from her and Cole knew the chasm between them was as wide as it had ever been.

"Damn it, why can't we? We're two consenting adults. We can be friends."

Sunshine threw her hands up in the air. "Friends?" She turned on her heel. "I'm going to bed."

"That's what I'm talking about. Let's go to bed. As buddies. Good buddies. We could be—"

She slammed the bathroom door and locked it.

"Partners." Cole trailed off. Damn it, that's what he should have led with. Partners. Why not? Why couldn't they share the building? The apartment, too.

A smile curved his mouth at that thought, but then he sobered again, realizing he'd blown it. Sunshine didn't want a fuck buddy. She didn't want a joint venture, either. She'd had her heart ripped out and handed to her by her last business partner. She wouldn't want to take that chance again.

It was either go all in or pull back and remain completely separate.

His head told him that keeping to himself was the smarter play—the business-like play.

But his heart hinted to him in the most unsettling way that throwing all in with Sunshine might be the best strategy he'd ever undertaken.

Chapter Thirteen

S O HE WANTED to sleep with her. Big surprise. That's what men did, right—sleep with every woman they could get their hands on? She remembered what Cab had said earlier, that she and Cole should work together. That was a non-starter; not when he was exactly like Greg. He'd use her as long as she had something to give him and dump her when he'd taken control of the building. She wouldn't make the same mistake twice.

The trouble was, Sunshine was attracted to Cole. What was wrong with her? Did she only fall for players?

She got ready for bed and when she exited the bathroom, her heart thumping in her chest, Cole was nowhere in sight. His bedroom door was shut, so she climbed into her makeshift bed on the couch and tried to fall asleep. After all, she had another busy day tomorrow. Hopefully she'd actually have some customers.

When she got up the following morning she felt like she'd been hit by a truck sometime in the intervening hours. It had taken her a long time to fall to sleep.

Whenever she'd closed her eyes, Cole's face had come to mind. His body, too. Try as she might to think of something else, the idea of sex with him kept insinuating itself into her thoughts.

Sex with Cole might be a heck of a lot of fun. He had a body it would be a pleasure to run her hands over. A mouth she already knew was a pleasure to kiss. She was sure that other interesting parts of Cole would be just as pleasurable to get to know. The ache of desire had kept her tossing and turning far too late into the night.

She hoped to get out of the apartment before he even woke up that morning, but when she cracked open the bathroom door after her shower and raced to the living room to retrieve the bra she'd forgotten to bring in with her, she was only halfway there when Cole walked out of the kitchen in his boxer briefs.

"Morning," he grunted, taking his time to look her up and down.

Sunshine grabbed the bra, whirled around and bolted for the bathroom. With the door shut behind her once more, she wanted to cry. This was impossible. All of it. What had Cecily been thinking?

As much as she loved her aunt, she found it hard to feel anything but anger toward her now. Did she really need this on top of everything that had gone before? Couldn't she have a short period of peace and ease before life handed her another set of problems?

No, she decided as she finished dressing and surveyed her reflection in the mirror. *You are not destined for an easy life. It's your lot to work and work and have men do their best to destroy you. So don't mix love and business, for heaven's sake. That way when the next man bails on you, at least you'll have a roof over your head.*

BY THE TIME Cole walked in the door, Sunshine was all set to open for the day. He had to hand it to her. The café looked cozy and inviting—an eclectic space that seemed to promise interesting food. The whole place was neat as a pin, the counter and tabletops gleaming. But thirty minutes later, not a single customer had come in to eat.

Not a single customer had come to the range, either.

Cole checked his watch. Strange. Usually someone had popped around by now. He decided to update his books but that didn't take too long and was far too depressing to spend much time on. The truth was he didn't make much of an income with the rifle range. His accounts made that all too clear. Maybe Sunshine was right; maybe he did need to branch out and start something online. But when he went online to check gun videos out, he quickly realized there were far too many of them available already.

"Slow day, huh?"

He nearly jumped when Sunshine spoke. She'd been so quiet since he arrived he'd forgotten he wasn't alone.

"You could say that."

"I need a real sign for the door, but I'm not sure it's worth the money if no one's going to come anyway." She leaned on her counter, her head turned his way. He leaned on his own counter.

"You got to have some patience."

"I know." She spread her hands wide. "But what if it doesn't work? What if I lose? I don't know what I'll do next. Go work for some other asshole, I guess."

He hated to hear her sound so discouraged. "What would you do if you could do anything in the whole world?"

"Anything?" She thought this over. "Forget it. You'll think it's dumb."

"Try me."

"I'd like to travel all over the world and see how other people cook. Not just at fancy restaurants, either, but how indigenous people cook, you know? Because I figure there has to be something to learn. If people with few resources and limited access to things like grocery stores and so on can make dishes that taste amazing, then we should be able to learn from that. I have this theory—" She broke off. "You don't want to hear all this."

"I do." He gestured to the empty room. "Even if I didn't, what else am I going to do until customers show up?" He was grateful that she was talking to him at all after last night. He'd really screwed up when he'd offered to jump in the sack with her. Now she thought he was just another guy trying to get one over on her.

Sunshine hesitated.

"I really do want to know," he assured her. "It sounds like you're on to something there." She'd certainly hit on a passion of his: travel. Not that he'd ever had much opportunity to do so, except in the military.

"I have this theory about simplicity. About how fancy dishes are great, but that a true chef can take a few simple ingredients and create something delicious from them. Know what I mean? And I think that studying indigenous food is the way to learn that."

"You could do one of those fancy cookbooks, too. Those travel cookbooks with lots of photographs." He'd seen them in bookstores and been interested, more for the photographs of far off places than for the recipes.

She made a face. "I'm a lousy photographer."

"You could take me along." He snapped his mouth shut. Why on earth had he said that?

But Sunshine seemed intrigued. "You do food photography, too? That landscape of yours is amazing."

She'd noticed it, huh? Cole felt exposed. "I've never photographed food, but I enjoy a challenge."

"Can I see some of your work?"

She moved around the counter and came to stand near him, as if he had a portfolio with him. Which actually, he did. In the apartment.

Now it was his turn to demur. "They're nothing special."

"Come on, go get a few photographs and bring them back. I'll hold down the fort until you do." She cast a sardonic glance around the empty room.

He allowed himself to be bullied into fetching the photographs. He hadn't shown them to many people.

He kept telling himself he was waiting for the perfect time before he tried to exhibit them anywhere. Besides, they weren't good enough for that. He was still learning.

When he returned, he paused just outside the front door, portfolio in hand, filled with misgivings. Of all the people to show his work to, his rival in the race to win this building certainly wasn't the smartest pick.

But when Sunshine spotted him through the glass door, she visibly brightened, which tugged him right through it before he could make up his mind to turn around. She beckoned him over to her larger counter and pushed things aside to make space. Taking the portfolio right out of his hands, she unzipped it and spread it wide, gasping in pleasure at the first photograph. It was a landscape of a ranch whose pastures spread out far and wide to the mountain range in the far distance. The warm tones of the close grasses contrasted sharply with the cool, far mountains. A stormy sky increased the drama of the photograph.

"Everyone takes pictures like these," he said, uncomfortable under her scrutiny of his work.

"It's so beautiful. Is it local?"

"That's right. It's a spread south of town. I could take you there sometime."

"I've only ever been in the town so far. It didn't occur to me it looked like this on the ranches."

"The local ranches have some of the best scenery I ever laid eyes on."

She turned to a new photograph. This one was of a stray dog that used to hang around the range until one of his customers took pity on it and gave it a home. In the photo the dog had the kind of downtrodden yet hopeful look that only an animal can pull off. Sunshine's expression melted in a way that told him he'd nailed that shot. The next was a photo of the apartments he owned, with old William leaning against one of the buildings, obviously killing time with nowhere to go. She bent over this one. "You've managed to make the buildings beautiful. It makes me think that even though they're plain and ordinary, they're important, because of the people they shelter."

"That's just how I feel about them."

She looked at him questioningly.

"I own them," he found himself admitting. "Before you get all excited, let me say that they don't make me a dime. Not right now, anyway."

"Why do you keep them?"

"Because of William there. Because of Tracey, our waitress at the diner the other night, and Scott Preston, a veteran buddy of mine. If I sold them, they'd lose their homes."

Sunshine nodded slowly and turned the page, but he had a feeling she was thinking over what he'd said. She kept leafing through his photos and he found that watching her face was a clear way to determine his prowess with his camera. By the end of her perusal he felt more confident in his abilities than he ever had before.

"There aren't any shots of food, though," she teased him.

"We can fix that. Put together a plate. I'll be right back."

When he returned a few minutes later, Sunshine had ladled out a bowl of her chili and tucked a slice of cornbread on the plate beside it.

"That's a good start," he said, checking the image on his camera. "But the counter doesn't make it stand out much."

Sunshine thought a minute. "How about this?" She brought out a bright yellow tablecloth, draped it over the counter and set the dishes on top of it.

Cole looked again. "That makes the chili pop, but the bread disappears."

"What color should I use then?"

Cole shrugged. He'd never studied this kind of thing formally. He simply went on instinct.

"We'll just have to try until we find something then."

Over the next five minutes, Sunshine dug out everything she could find that might make a suitable backdrop. In the end a dark green cloth made both the chili and the cornbread shine.

"Got any Parmesan cheese?"

"Soy Parmesan." She went and grabbed some.

Cole read the label, shook his head, but decided it would do. He shook the canister a couple of times, dotting the surface of the chili with the fake cheese in an artful half-moon shape. "Got to give the image some motion—something to draw the eye."

He took a few shots. Tried a different angle, then

took some more. When he was done, he let Sunshine look through them.

"Wow—these look great. Can you send them to me so I can use them on my website?"

"Sure thing." He frowned. Wait—now he was helping her again.

She must have had the same thought. "Why don't we go take photos of the range, too? You can add them to the website I made for you."

He supposed that was something.

Sunshine tidied away the food and followed him into the range, since they still had no customers. Cole spent several minutes taking shots from various directions, but it was clear almost from the first that the photos would be duds.

"What's wrong?" Sunshine asked when he stopped taking pictures.

"The light's awful in here and there's nothing to make it interesting. I need people. Action."

"You could photograph me."

"Holding a firearm?"

She blinked, but then nodded. "Sure. Why not?"

"It won't be loaded," he assured her.

"Pity." But she flashed him a smile. Sunshine obviously was enjoying this creative activity. He was enjoying it too, mostly because of the company. His photography had always been a solitary experience before now.

"Now if you were wearing a bikini, we'd really pack them in." He gathered up three types of firearms, a pistol, a shotgun and an AK-47.

"Really?" She laughed.

"I'm not joking."

"Huh." Sunshine thought a minute. "Hang on!" She ran for the door.

While he waited, Cole worked to set up the shot. He didn't believe for a minute she'd return in a bikini, but he hoped she'd find something a little bit sexy. He moved things around to have less clutter in the frame and found an extra lamp in the storage room to brighten up the area. By the time Sunshine got back he was ready for her.

But he wasn't ready for the outfit she had on.

Chapter Fourteen

SUNSHINE BIT HER lip. Had she gone too far? She wasn't sure what had possessed her to slip into the slinkiest outfit she could put together—a barely there skirt she used to wear out dancing and a plunging halter top she normally wore as a cover-up at the beach. She had no idea if she was playing along with his sick male fantasy of a hot girl with a big gun—or if she simply wanted to grab hold of Cole's attention and make sure he knew exactly what she had to offer.

At some point this morning things had shifted and she'd gone from thinking of him as her enemy, to feeling like he could be a good friend. Maybe it was that they were both in the same position—competing for a chance to continue with their dream.

Or maybe it was that he was the handsomest cowboy she'd ever met, and her body wanted to get closer to his.

She wanted him to look at her, she decided. It was as simple as that.

She wanted him to want her.

A dangerous look came into Cole's eyes when she

walked in. He put down the camera and crossed the room to her.

Sunshine took a step back.

"Don't even think of running away." He took her hand. "Hell, woman. You're lethal in that outfit."

His back-country compliment warmed her all over. "You're just saying that."

"No, I'm definitely not just saying that." He hesitated long enough that she thought he might pull her in and kiss her again the way he had before, but after a moment he let her go. Was that regret she saw in his eyes?

"I'll show you. Come here." He led her to the shooting range, sat her on the edge of the one of counters that demarked a gallery, and handed her an unloaded AK-47. "Smile for the camera."

Sunshine did. Her naughtiest, come-hither-est smile.

"That's it," Cole said. "Come on, baby, sell it."

Sunshine burst out laughing. "Sorry. Sorry! It's just too silly."

"Nothing silly about sex and guns, baby. Try it again." For several minutes he bossed her around, but she couldn't stop giggling. "Let's take a break," Cole said. "Need a glass of water?"

"Yes, please." While he was gone she pulled herself together, knowing that most of her laughter was just nerves. No man had ever looked at her the way Cole was looking at her—both as a man and as an artist. Submitting herself to his orders felt more intimate than just about anything else they could do.

When he returned with her drink, his fingers touched hers when he handed it to her. She swallowed, her throat suddenly dry. "I think I'm ready now."

"Good." His gaze was bright and shining with mischief. "Let's try again."

THIS TIME SUNSHINE was more serious, and while he appreciated that she was no longer giggling, Cole missed the vivacity of her laugh. He wondered if he could harness both Sunshine's intrinsic sexiness and the silliness of what they were doing. He had a feeling if he could get it right, the resulting image would sucker-punch just about every man in the grand state of Montana, and they'd all come flocking to his range.

He had to make Sunshine forget she was posing for a camera. How could he do that? "I want to see some muscles." Sunshine did her best, and the results made her chuckle, but it wasn't enough. For a while they tried different poses and different guns, but he couldn't get the shot he was trying for.

"I'm getting tired," she said. "And cold."

"Cold? It's the middle of the summer. I'm burning up. Just a few more shots. Go back to the AK."

"Fine." She picked up the gun, sat on the counter and crossed her bare legs in front of her.

"Hold it right," he told her and she gripped the weapon as if about to shoot it. "Show me some cleavage, honey."

She rolled her eyes and plumped up her breasts under her halter top. Leaning forward, she shimmied her shoulders until Cole shifted, feeling a stirring of something down south of his belt. "Damn, it's really hot in here now." He smiled at her, then in one smooth motion reached behind his head and peeled off his T-shirt, knowing she liked that move. He held up the camera again, edging closer.

"Wooh, who's showing some skin now?" she said.

"I'll show you some skin," he said, his voice deep and suggestive. One handed, still holding the camera up to take the shot, he fumbled with his belt buckle and dropped his pants. "Come on, baby. Pose like this." He did an over-the-top cheesecake pose that had Sunshine cracking up. "No? You don't like that? How about this?" He pulled another crazy pose, balanced on a single leg.

Sunshine tossed her head back and laughed. Before she could recover Cole snapped a half-dozen shots. She held up a hand. "Stop it. I'll look like an ass."

"What the hell are you two doing?"

Sunshine jumped off the counter and Cole spun around.

Holt Matheson stood gaping at them in the doorway. The rest of Cole's friends stood right behind him.

Well, hell, this was embarrassing. Cole awkwardly pulled up his jeans, zipped and buckled them, his camera still in his hand. "You all ever heard of knocking?"

"Never had to knock before." Holt stood his ground. "Never caught you prancing around in your skivvies, either."

Jamie wolf-whistled as he pushed past the older man and stepped inside. "Sunshine, you look hot! You posing for a calendar or something?"

Sunshine's cheeks were scarlet, but she took her cue from Cole and set her firearm down carefully on the counter. "Not a calendar, some promotional photos to help drum up more business for Cole."

"Why the hell would you do that? Thought you two were enemies," Holt said.

"More business for Cole means more business for me," Sunshine said. "And maybe most of the customers will be too enticed by my food to even make it into the range."

"They'll be enticed by something, but it won't be your cooking, I'll tell you that," Holt said with a significant look at her skimpy outfit. Sunshine flinched at the insult, and crossed her arms over her chest.

"Everybody out!" Cole knew he might be alienating his best customers as he said it, but he couldn't stand the look on Sunshine's face or the way she'd caved in on herself. If Holt Matheson thought he could come in here and insult his girl he had another—

His thoughts crashed together. His girl? When had Sunshine become his girl? But his body was functioning on automatic pilot and he ushered the whole crowd out of the range and shut the door behind them.

"You don't have to do that."

"Like hell I don't." Cole caught Sunshine as she headed for the door, too. "Holt Matheson is a cranky old man. Don't you listen to him. You are the most beautiful woman to hit Chance Creek for years. You have nothing to be ashamed about."

"Prancing around with guns—in a sleazy outfit? Sure I do." She tried to get past him again.

"That's not sleazy. That's sexy. There's a big difference. Listen." He took her by the arms, enjoying her soft skin under his fingers all too much. "We won't use the photographs unless you want me to. We'll figure out something else. But I hope you'll let me keep them to look at on my own time."

She turned her head, but he cupped her chin in one hand and brought her back to look at him. "Hey. If I could look like that in a photo and some woman wanted to keep it to ogle now and then? I'd do it in a heartbeat."

"Oh, yeah?" Now she was smiling again.

"Yeah."

"So you'll go and pose with those guns and let me photograph you?"

Cole swallowed. "I said I'd do that if some woman wanted to ogle me now and then."

"I might want to ogle you now and then."

"Well, hell, that's different." Cole unbuckled his jeans, made quick work of the button and zipper and kicked them all the way off. Hooking his thumbs in the waistband of his boxer briefs, he added, "You want these bad boys off too?"

"I think we better keep it tame for now."

From the way her gaze was locked on his boxer briefs, though, he was sure she was more than a little interested about what was going on underneath. What was going on underneath was a direct response to her sexy outfit. Pretty soon, tame was not going to describe this encounter.

He willed himself into a more presentable state—he didn't need raunchy photos of himself all over the Internet—and positioned the AK strategically. If the photos found their way into the public's hands, let them ogle his thighs and biceps, not his—

"Looking good," Sunshine crooned, taking up the camera and holding it up to take a shot. "Sell it to me, baby."

Cole did his best, although it was only moments before his bravado faded and it became more work than play. He was relieved when Sunshine put the camera down. "Okay, you're off the hook. You're a good sport."

"You're a good sport, too. Let's get these photos downloaded and off my camera. We'll go through them together and get rid of any ones we don't want."

"Thanks."

Chapter Fifteen

SUNSHINE HADN'T COUNTED on the men still waiting in the café for them, but when they walked through the range door, Holt, Ethan, Jamie, Rob and Cab were all there.

"Good to see you got your clothes back on, Cole," Holt said. "Thought I might go blind a minute there."

"I'm glad *you* didn't change," Jamie said to Sunshine. "I like your outfit."

"Well, I don't like having to wait forty minutes to place my order," Holt said.

Sunshine, on her way toward the door, stopped in surprise. "You're going to order?"

"If I can ever get any service around here."

She really wanted to go and change before anyone else happened by, but Sunshine figured that a customer was a customer. If the ornery old man was actually going to eat here, she'd better jump on the opportunity. She turned around, went to the counter and grabbed her order pad. "What'll you have?"

"Rob's been yammering on about some chili. Says it's pretty good. Now I see he's been too distracted by the scenery to even taste it."

"Dad—Sunshine was wearing clothes last time." Rob wiped a hand over his jaw. "I mean, not that you aren't now. Well, at least some—"

"What Rob's trying to say is the chili is good." Cole whacked Rob on the arm.

"How would you know? You've never tried any," Sunshine said.

Cole scratched the back of his neck and she wondered if he'd just remembered they were supposed to be on opposite sides. They didn't feel like they were enemies anymore, though.

"Well, it smells good, anyway."

"I'll bring you both a bowl."

The others placed orders too, and Sunshine went happily to fix them up, forgetting about her clothing for a while. When the bells chimed to announce another customer, she looked up to smile broadly in welcome to the newcomer.

The unfamiliar man blinked, then grinned back. He spotted Cole. "Hey, man. I like what you've done to the place."

Feeling self-conscious all over again, Sunshine grabbed a menu, then put it back. This man wasn't here to eat—he was here to shoot, if the case in his hand was any indication.

"Come on back, Bud," Cole said.

"I don't know, Cole. Some food sounds pretty good right about now."

"We're having chili," Holt said.

"Chili will do just fine." Bud sat down with the other men. He was middle aged, with thinning hair and heavy features. His gaze followed Sunshine's every move.

"One bowl of chili, coming right up," Sunshine said, and wished there was a door through the kitchen straight into the apartment. Maybe Cole could do something about that one of these days. She tugged her neckline higher and went behind the counter to see to the food. Several minutes later, when she was ready to serve it, she turned back to find Bud still eyeing her.

She wasn't the only one who had noticed. Cole was watching the man watch her, and she wasn't sure how to take that. She had a feeling Bud was treading on thin ice.

She efficiently hefted the tray of bowls and made her way to the table. Handing them around, she checked to make sure everyone had the proper silverware and enough vegan spread for the cornbread.

"Honey, looks like you dropped a fork over there," Bud said.

She turned to scan the floor, but saw nothing. "Where?"

"Under that table. Way under."

Sunshine bent to look and heard the unmistakable sound of a camera app on a cell phone click behind her. She straightened quickly and spun around. "What do you think you're doing?"

She knew what he was doing—snapping a photo of her bottom in her tight micro mini—but before she could snatch his phone away, Cole beat her to it, dropped it on the floor and smashed it with the heel of his boot.

"What the hell?" Bud stood up, his chair scraping across the floor.

"Out!"

"But—"

"Out—consider yourself banned!"

"Cole!"

But Cole wasn't kidding around and Bud figured that out pretty quickly, especially when a look around the table showed him that no one was on his side.

"I ain't paying for that chili." He stormed across the room and out the door.

"That's more business you just lost," Holt said when he was gone. "Kind of on a roll, aren't you?"

"Shut up."

"Testy, too," Holt observed to the others.

"You all right?" Cole asked Sunshine.

"I'm fine." In fact, she was more than fine. The ferocity with which Cole had defended her made her feel more protected than she'd felt in years. He'd kicked out a customer—a customer whose business he needed— for her sake. That told her he cared about her more than anything he might have said. A tendril of happiness curled through her. Maybe things were looking up. But she still needed to get out of here and change. When she and Cole were alone the sexiness of her outfit had been playful. Now it was simply embarrassing. "Can you hold the fort while I go put on something else?"

"Sure. I'll walk with you and make sure Bud's not loitering around."

Cole walked her all the way to the apartment and stayed there until she was safely inside. When she moved to close the door behind her, he followed her inside. "Mind if I watch?"

The playfulness was back, as was the buzz she felt all through her veins. She knew if she said no, Cole would make out that his request was just a joke and would return to the range. She didn't want to say no, though. She wanted Cole to watch her. She wanted him to touch her, too, but that would have to wait until later.

She nodded.

Cole's eyebrows rose in surprise, but he shut the door behind him with alacrity, and leaned against it, never taking his gaze from her. Without a word, she found her clothes from earlier and laid them out on the couch. First she untied her halter top and let it fall away. A hiss of breath told her Cole found what he saw to his liking. She took her time reaching down and shimmying out of her skirt, pulling off her panties for good measure. Why not? In for a penny, in for a pound. She found she wasn't shy in front of Cole. She knew he appreciated the view. Knew too he wanted to touch her as badly as she wanted to be touched. She let him get a good long look before reaching for the soft, floor-length skirt she'd started the day in.

"You aren't going to wear anything underneath that?

She shook her head. "And I want you to think about that all day long."

He groaned. "You're killing me."

"Don't die yet, cowboy. I've got plans for you later." She pulled on a pretty bra and fastened it behind her, then slipped on her shirt.

"What kind of plans?" He reached for her as she made her way to the door.

"Good ones." She reached up on tip-toes and kissed him square on the mouth. He caught her in his arms and returned the favor.

"Guess I'd better get back to the range," he said some minutes later.

"I'll be there in a minute."

"Good."

Chapter Sixteen

THE REST OF the day dragged for Cole, even though business picked up late in the afternoon. Sunshine even got some customers during the dinner hour, including several single men who sidled through the door, peering around with great interest until they located her and saw she was fully clothed. Cole could tell that Bud had been talking.

His violent reaction to the man's attempt to photograph Sunshine's ass had surprised him, especially when he considered that he had been doing almost the same thing just a few minutes before.

That was different, he told himself. Sunshine had agreed to it, for one thing, and she'd posed herself, but he had to admit he'd taken the pictures for the same reason Bud had—he wanted to look at her body later when he was alone.

The view Sunshine had given him when they went back to the apartment had been far better than any of the photographs he'd taken earlier, though, and she'd as good as promised they'd be together tonight.

By the time they closed up, Sunshine seemed satisfied with her day and Cole was aching—physically aching—to get her alone. He knew he needed to watch his step, but his body wasn't going to let him take things too slow.

"Word about my restaurant is spreading," she announced happily as they walked the short distance to their apartment.

Cole didn't say what he was thinking—that most of her customers today came to see her rather than eat her food. At the very least none of them had disliked her cooking. He had to admit her chili wasn't half-bad. A little beef in there wouldn't have hurt, but he'd hardly missed it.

He wanted to ease into things slowly when they let themselves into the apartment, but they'd barely stepped into the living room when Sunshine turned to say something, bumped into him since he was trailing so close behind, and his arms went around her of their own accord. An instant later he was kissing her again. God, he couldn't get enough of kissing Sunshine. With a sigh, she melted against him and he drew her close, one hand cupping the base of her head, the other sliding down over the curve of her hip.

A few minutes later, he pulled back.

"I've been waiting all day to do that."

"Oh, yeah?"

"Yeah." He did it again and kept kissing her until both of them were breathless. He began to angle her toward the sofa and lowered her down, positioning himself on top of her.

She didn't fight him. Instead, she kissed him back, twining her arms around his neck. When he reached a hand under her soft cotton shirt, she pulled back and for one awful second Cole thought she would stop him. Instead, she lifted it slowly over her head. Her silky, pretty bra tantalized him, and he dropped appreciative kisses along the edge of the fabric, his mouth brushing her soft curves. He had fun teasing her for some time before he found the clasp behind her back and freed her to his view.

"Magnificent," he said, bending down to take one nipple into his mouth. Sunshine moaned and arched her back, the better to give him access as he teased and played with her, lavishing attention on first one, then the other breast.

It was obvious she loved his touch and that fueled the fire within him even more. She'd been so distant when she arrived, he'd thought she was forever out of his reach. To find that not only would she allow him to be close to her, but that she wanted it so badly revved him just thinking about it.

When she grew restless, he took her hand, led her to the bedroom and shut the door. He sat down on the bed and drew her down to lay beside him. He shifted on top of her and soon moved his hands to the waistband of her floor-length skirt. It was soft and stretchy, skimming her hips and flaring at the hem. It made her look like some sort of goddess, but he decided it too needed to go.

He wanted all of her.

He slid his hands under the waistband, loving that she'd let him know earlier that she wore nothing beneath. He'd never be able to watch her in the café again without wondering what she had on. As he slid the skirt over her hips, his hands caressing her ass as he did so, Sunshine moaned again, and Cole wanted to join her. She was so beautiful and so open to him. He wouldn't have believed it a week ago if someone told him they'd be together like this. He put all thoughts of the past and future behind him and bent to the task of making Sunshine moan again.

He moved to trail kisses down her belly and between her legs, gently parting them for better access. Sunshine opened to his touch and sighed when he explored her most intimate places. She ran her hands over his shoulders, urging him on by lifting her hips. When she began to grip him hard, he knew she was close.

Heat flooded him at the idea of being inside her. He was so hard he ached, but he knew he was moments from getting everything he wanted, and he didn't mind taking it slow.

He stood up. "Be right back." He paced across to the bathroom, knowing she was watching him and hoping she like what she saw. When he returned, he grinned at her expression and she smiled devilishly back at him. She took the condom out of his hand when he approached and he steeled himself for the sweet torture of her putting it on him. Her hands running over the length of his hardness nearly had him coming undone, but when he laid her back down on the bed and positioned himself above her, it was all worth it to know what would come next.

"Why are you looking at me like that?" she asked.

"Because I want to remember everything." Cole couldn't wait another moment. He lowered himself down on top of her and pressed inside, both of them moaning together.

Cole's rhythm was uneven at first because he was so turned on he was having trouble holding back, but they found their groove and soon both of them were breathing hard. Sunshine was unbelievably slick and hot, taking him to heights he hadn't ever felt before. She was unashamed of showing her reactions and her cries and moans teased him until he could hardly hold back. When she wrapped her legs around his waist, it was all over. He thrust into her hard and fast until both of them cried out in unison. After a short interval, they joined together more slowly, exploring each other more thoroughly, until Cole's long, strong strokes brought Sunshine over the edge again.

When they lay entwined together, Cole stroking Sunshine from shoulder to hip, Sunshine running her fingers over his chest, she asked, "Now what do we do?"

"We could do it again."

She swatted him playfully. "I mean with the restaurant and rifle range."

He thought about that. "We work together, I guess. There's no reason why we can't share, is there?"

"Not as long as we're together," she said slowly.

He turned to her in surprise. "You thinking about going somewhere?"

"No. But I hardly know you. Maybe you're all about one-night stands."

He was sure she had to see in his eyes that wasn't true—not this time. "I think we've got something special." He touched her cheek. "I don't think I'm going to let you go."

A smile curved her mouth. "I'm glad to hear it. What'll we call it though?"

"The building? How about Sunshine's Café and Rifle Range?"

She sat up. "It's not my rifle range."

"Yeah, but your name is cooler than mine."

"I swore I wouldn't do this again—mix business with pleasure."

"I'm not Greg," he assured her. "I swear I won't let you down. In fact, I swear someday I'll take you on that trip around the world, Sunshine."

"Really?"

"Really."

"Living and working together seems pretty serious for two people who just met."

"Normally I'd agree with you, but not this time."

"What makes this time different?" She gasped as he swept a kiss down her jaw and under her chin.

"You." He pulled back to face her. "I won't ever get tired of you." He shifted her back down on the pillows.

She sighed as he positioned himself over her. "You

think we've got what it takes for the long haul?"

"I think we'll have a lot of fun finding that out." He fished out another condom from his bedside table, made short work of sheathing himself, then surprised her by rolling over and pulling her on top of him. "Meanwhile we better make doubly sure we're compatible."

"Don't you mean triply sure?" she said, arching back as he filled her again.

"That too."

"What are all your friends going to say?" She gasped as Cole reached up, cupped her breasts and ran his hands over her sensitive nipples.

"They're going to wish like hell they were exactly where I am right now. But they won't get that chance, will they?"

"No." She shook her head until her long hair swirled around her body. Cole's hands dropped to her hips as he rocked inside her.

"It's just you and me now, isn't it?"

She nodded, arching her back and moving with him.

"No one else?"

"No one else."

They didn't speak again for a long, long time.

Chapter Seventeen

WHEN SUNSHINE WOKE the following morning, at first she couldn't remember where she was. She wasn't lying in her accustomed spot on the leather couch. Instead, she was curled up cozily in a large, comfortable bed.

"Good morning."

Cole's voice brought it all back and her cheeks warmed as she remembered the many and varied ways they'd been together the night before.

"Morning."

"I suppose we have to get up."

"I suppose we do."

The look in his eye told her he could think of better things to do, and she could too, but it was late and there might be customers waiting.

"Hold that thought until tonight," she said, and pressed a finger to his lips.

"If I have to," he grumbled, but climbed out of bed, giving her all too good of an idea just what had been on his mind. They met again five minutes later on the back deck. Coffee in hand, Sunshine stared across the empty field at the two apartment buildings.

"I guess we'll have to make sure we keep all those people afloat."

"We?"

She nodded. "We. I'll help. We'll do it together."

"I meant what I said last night, though," Cole said. "Someday we'll see the world together."

"I'm looking forward to that."

"Do you think this is what Cecily had in mind all the time?" he asked as he took her coffee cup from her, placed it on the railing and pulled her close again.

"Maybe." She twined her arms around his neck.

A half-hour later they stumbled around the corner to find Ethan and Rob already waiting by the door.

"It's about time," Ethan said. "I gotta improve my score."

"And I need some chili," Rob said. "And a vegetable. Gotta improve my score, too."

When both Sunshine and Cole laughed along with him, he eyed them suspiciously. "You two are awfully happy. What gives?"

"Nothing." Cole was firm. "Just another busy day."

They weren't fooling anyone, Sunshine realized later, however, when she heard Jamie tell Cab, "They're sleeping together. It's obvious. I don't know how Cole changed her mind."

"Maybe she changed his."

"Maybe we changed each other's," Cole said out loud, surprising all of them. "However it happened, Sunshine's off limits."

"So what happens when the four months are up?" Rob pressed. "Will you own the building or will Sunshine? Who's the winner?"

Cole took her hand, raised it and pressed a kiss into her palm. "We'll own it together and we'll both win, right Sunshine?"

"You got that right."

The **Cowboys of Chance Creek** series continues with **The Cowboy's E-Mail Order Bride**.

Be the first to know about Cora Seton's new releases! Sign up for her newsletter here!
www.coraseton.com/sign-up-for-my-newsletter

Reviews mean so much to authors! If you enjoyed **The Cowboy Inherits a Bride**, please consider leaving a review – even a short one!

Read on for an excerpt of **The Cowboy's E-Mail Order Bride**.

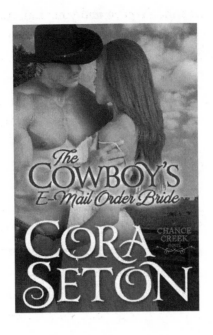

The
COWBOY'S
E-Mail Order Bride

CORA
SETON

CHANCE
CREEK
novel

Chapter One

"**Y**OU DID WHAT?" Ethan Cruz turned his back on the slate and glass entrance to Chance Creek, Montana's Regional Airport, and jiggled the door handle of Rob Matheson's battered red Chevy truck. Locked. It figured—Rob had to know he'd want to turn tail and head back to town the minute he found out what his friends had done. "Open the damned door, Rob."

"Not a chance. You've got to come in—we're picking up your bride."

"I don't have a bride and no one getting off that

plane concerns me. You've had your fun, now open up the door or I'm grabbing a taxi." He faced his friends. Rob, who'd lived on the ranch next door to his their entire lives. Cab Johnson, county sheriff, who was far too level-headed to be part of this mess. And Jamie Lassiter, the best horse trainer west of the Mississippi as long as you could pry him away from the ladies. The four of them had gone to school together, played football together, and spent more Saturday nights at the bar than he could count. How many times had he gotten them out of trouble, drove them home when they'd had one beer to many, listened to them bellyache about their girlfriends or lack thereof when all he really wanted to do was knock back a cold one and play a game of pool? What the hell had he ever done to deserve this?

Unfortunately, he knew exactly what he'd done. He'd played a spectacularly brilliant prank a month or so ago on Rob—a prank that still had the town buzzing—and Rob concocted this nightmare as payback. Rob got him drunk one night and egged him on about his ex-fiancee until he spilled his guts about how much it still bothered him that Lacey Taylor had given him the boot in favor of that rich sonofabitch Carl Whitfield. The name made him want to spit. Dressed like a cowboy when everyone knew he couldn't ride to save his life.

Lacey bailed on him just as life had delivered a walloping one-two punch. First his parents died in a car accident. Then he discovered the ranch was mortgaged to the hilt. As soon as Lacey learned there would be some hard times ahead, she took off like a runaway horse. Didn't even have the decency to break up with him face to face. Before he knew it Carl was flying Lacey all over creation in his private plane. Las Vegas. San Francisco. Houston. He never had a chance to get her back.

He should have kept his thoughts bottled up where they belonged—would have kept them bottled up if Rob hadn't kept putting those shots into his hand—but no, after he got done swearing and railing at Lacey's bad taste in men, he apparently decided to lecture his friends on the merits of a real woman. The kind of woman a cowboy should marry.

And Rob—good ol' Rob—captured the whole thing with his cell phone.

When he showed it to him the following day, Ethan made short work of the asinine gadget, but it was too late. Rob had already emailed the video to Cab and Jamie, and the three of them spent the next several days making his life damn miserable over it.

If only they'd left it there.

The other two would have, but Rob was still sore about that old practical joke, so he took things even further. He decided there must be a woman out there somewhere who met all of the requirements Ethan expounded on during his drunken rant. To find her, he did what any rational man would do. He edited Ethan's rant into a video advertisement for a damned mail order bride.

And posted it on YouTube.

Rob showed him the video on the ride over to the airport. There he was for all the world to see, sounding like a jack-ass—hell, looking like one, too. Rob's fancy editing made his rant sound like a proposition. "What I want," he heard himself say, "is a traditional bride. A bride for a cowboy. 18—25 years old, willing to work hard, beautiful, quiet, sweet, good cook, ready for children. I'm willing to give her a trial. One month'll tell me all I need to know." Then the image cut out to a screen full of text, telling women how to submit their video applications.

Unbelievable. This was low—real low—even for Rob.

Ready for children?

"You all are cracked in the head. I'm not going in there."

"Come on, Ethan," Cab said. The big man stood with his legs spread, his arms folded over his barrel chest, ready to stop him if he tried to run. "The girl's come all the way from New York. You're not even going to say hello? What kind of a fiance are you?"

He clenched his fists. "No kind at all. And there isn't any girl in there. You know it. I know it. So stop wasting my time. There isn't any girl dumb enough to answer something like that!"

The other men exchanged a look.

"Actually," Jamie said, leaning against the Chevy and rubbing the stubble on his chin with the back of his hand. "We got nearly 200 answers to that video. Took us hours to get through them all." He grinned. "Who can resist a cowboy, right?"

As far as Ethan was concerned, plenty of women could. Lacey certainly had resisted him. Hence his bachelor status. "So you picked the ugliest, dumbest girl and tricked her into buying a plane ticket. Terrific."

Rob looked pained. "No, we found one that's both hot and smart. And we chipped in and bought the ticket—round trip, because we figured you wouldn't know a good thing when it kicked you in the butt, so we'd have to send her back. Have a little faith in your friends. You think we'd steer you wrong?"

Hell, yes. Ethan took a deep breath and squared his shoulders. The guys wouldn't admit they were joking until he'd gone into the airport and hung around the gate looking foolish for a suitable amount of time. And if they were stupid enough to actually fly a girl out here, he couldn't trust them to put her back on a plane home. So now instead of finishing his chores before supper, he'd lose the rest of the afternoon sorting out this mess.

"Fine. Let's get this over with," he said, striding toward the front door. Inside, he didn't bother to look at the television screen which showed incoming and outgoing flights. Chance Creek Regional had all of four gates. He'd just follow the hall as far as homeland security allowed him and wait until some lost soul deplaned.

"Look—it's on time." Rob grabbed his arm and tried to hurry him along. Ethan dug in the heels of his well worn boots and proceeded at his own pace.

Jamie pulled a cardboard sign out from under his

jacket and flashed it at Ethan before holding it up above his head. It read, Autumn Leeds. Jamie shrugged at Ethan's expression. "I know—the name's brutal."

"Want to see her?" Cab pulled out a gadget and handed it over. Ethan held it gingerly. The laptop he bought on the advice of his accountant still sat untouched in his tiny office back at the ranch. He hated these miniature things that ran on swoops and swipes and taps on buttons that weren't really there. Cab reached over and pressed something and it came to life, showing a pretty young woman in a cotton dress in a kitchen preparing what appeared to be a pot roast.

"Hi, I'm Autumn," she said, looking straight at him. "Autumn Leeds. As you can see, I love cooking…"

Rob whooped and pointed. "Look—there she is! I told you she'd come!"

Ethan raised his gaze from the gadget to see the woman herself walking toward them down the carpeted hall. Long black hair, startling blue eyes, porcelain-white skin, she was thin and haunted and luminous all at the same time. She, too, held a cell phone and seemed to be consulting it, her gaze glancing down then sweeping the crowd. As their eyes met, hers widened with recognition. He groaned inwardly when he realized this pretty woman had probably watched Rob's stupid video multiple times. She might be looking at his picture now.

As the crowd of passengers and relatives split around their party, she walked straight up to them and held out her hand. "Ethan Cruz?" Her voice was low and husky, her fingers cool and her handshake firm. He found himself wanting to linger over it. Instead he nodded. "I'm Autumn Leeds. Your bride."

AUTUMN HAD NEVER BEEN more terrified in her life. In her short career as a columnist for CityPretty Magazine, she'd interviewed models, society women, CEO's and politicians, but all of them were urbanites, and she'd never had to leave New York to get the job done. As soon as her plane departed LaGuardia she knew she'd made a mistake. As the city skyline fell away and the countryside below her emptied into farmland, she clutched the arms of her seat as if she was heading for the moon rather than Montana. Now, hours later, she felt off-kilter and fuzzy, and the four men before her looked like extras in a Western flick. Large, muscled, rough men who all exuded a distinct odor of sweat she realized probably came from an honest afternoon's work. Entirely out of her comfort zone, she wondered for the millionth time if she'd done the right thing. It's the only way to get my contract renewed, she reminded herself. She had to write a story different from all the other articles in CityPretty. In these tough economic times, the magazine was downsizing—again. If she didn't want to find herself out on the street, she had to produce—fast.

And what better story to write than the tale of a Montana cowboy using YouTube to search for an email-order bride?

Ethan Cruz looked back at her, seemingly at a loss for words. Well, that was to be expected with a cowboy, right? The ones in movies said about one word every ten minutes or so. That's why his video said she needed to be quiet. Well, she could be quiet. She didn't trust herself to speak, anyway.

She'd never been so near a cowboy before. Her best friend, Becka, helped shoot her video response, and they'd spent a hilarious day creating a pseudo-Autumn guaranteed to warm the cockles of a cowboy's heart. Together, they'd decided to pitch her as desperate to escape the dirty city and unleash her inner farm wife on Ethan's Montana ranch. They hinted she loved gardening, canning, and all the domestic arts. They played up both her toughness (she played first base in high school baseball) and her femininity (she loved quilting—*what an outright lie*). She had six costume changes in the three minute video.

Over her vehement protests, Becka forced her to end the video with a close-up of her face while she uttered the words, "I often fall asleep imagining the family I'll someday have." Autumn's cheeks warmed as she recalled the depth of the deception. She wasn't a country girl pining to be a wife; she was a career girl who didn't intend to have kids for at least another decade. Right?

Of course.

Except somehow, when she watched the final video, the life the false Autumn said she wanted sounded far more compelling than the life the real Autumn lived. Especially the part about wanting a family.

It wasn't that she didn't want a career. She just wanted a different one—a different life. She hated how hectic and shallow everything seemed now. She remembered her childhood, back when she had two parents—a successful investment banker father and a stay-at-home mother who made the best cookies in New York City. Back then, her mom, Teresa, loved to take Autumn and her sister, Lily, to visit museums, see movies and plays, walk in Central Park and shop in the ethnic groceries that surrounded their home. On Sundays, they cooked fabulous feasts together and her mother's laugh rang out loud and often. Friends and relatives stopped by to eat and talk, and Autumn played with the other children while the grownups clustered around the kitchen table. All that changed when she turned nine and her father left them for a travel agent. Her parents' divorce was horrible. The fight wasn't over custody; her father was all too eager to leave child-rearing to her mother while he toured Brazil with his new wife. The fight was over money—over the bulk of the savings her father had transferred to offshore accounts in the weeks before the breakup, and refused to return.

Broke, single and humiliated, her mother took up the threads of the life she'd put aside to marry and raise a family. A graduate of an elite liberal arts college, with several years of medical school already under her belt, she moved them into a tiny apartment on the edge of a barely-decent neighborhood and returned to her studies. Those were lean, lonely years when everyone had to pitch in. Autumn's older sister watched over her after school, and Teresa expected them to take on any and all chores they could possibly handle. As Autumn grew, she took over the cooking and shopping and finally the family's accounts. Teresa had no time for cultural excursions, let alone entertaining friends, but by the time Autumn was ready to go to college herself, she ran a successful OB-GYN practice that catered to wealthy women who'd left childbearing until the last possible moment, and she didn't even have to take out a loan to fund her education.

Determined her daughters would never face the same challenges she had, Teresa raised them with three guiding precepts:

Every woman must be self-supporting.

Marriage is a trap set by men for women.

Parenthood must be postponed until one reaches the pinnacle of her career.

Autumn's sister, Lily, was a shining example of this guide to life. She was single, ran her own physical therapy clinic, and didn't plan to marry or have children any time soon. Next to her, Autumn felt like a black sheep. She couldn't seem to accept work was all there was to life. Couldn't forget the joy of laying a table for a host of guests. She still missed those happy, crowded Sunday afternoons so much it hurt her to think about them.

She forced her thoughts back to the present. The man before her was ten times more handsome than he was in his video, and that was saying a lot. Dark hair, blue eyes, a chiseled jaw with just a trace of manly stubble. His shoulders were broad and his stance radiated a determination she found more than compelling. This was a man you could lean on, a man who could take care of the bad guys, wrangle the cattle, and still sweep you off your feet.

"Ethan, aren't you going to say hello to your fiancee?" One of the other men stuck out his hand. "I'm Rob Matheson. This is Cab Johnson and Jamie Lassiter. Ethan here needed some backup."

Rob was blonde, about Ethan's size, but not nearly so serious. In fact, she bet he was a real cut-up. That shit-eating grin probably never left his face. Cab was larger than the others—six foot four maybe, powerfully built. He wore a sheriff's uniform. Jamie was lean but muscular, with dark brown hair that fell into his eyes. They had the easy camaraderie that spoke of a long acquaintance. They probably knew each other as kids, and would take turns being best man at each other's weddings.

Her wedding.

No—she'd be long gone before the month was up. She had three weeks to turn in the story; maybe four, if it was really juicy. She'd pitched it to the editor of CityPretty as soon as the idea occurred to her. Margaret's uncertain approval told her she was probably allowing her one last hurrah before CityPretty let her go.

Still, just for one moment she imagined herself standing side by side Ethan at the altar of some country church, pledging her love to him. What would it be like to marry a near stranger and try to forge a life with him?

Insane, that's what.

So why did the idea send tendrils of warmth into all the right places?

She glanced up at Ethan to find him glancing down, and the warm feeling curved around her insides again.

Surely New York men couldn't be shorter than this crew, or any less manly, but she couldn't remember the last time she'd been around so much blatant testosterone. She must be ovulating. Why else would she react like this to a perfect stranger?

Ethan touched her arm. "This way." She followed him down the hall, the others falling into place behind them like a cowboy entourage. She stifled a sudden laugh at the absurdity of it all, slipped her hand into her purse and grabbed her digital camera, capturing the scene with a few clicks. Had this man—this...*cowboy*—sat down and planned out the video he'd made? She tried to picture Ethan bending over a desk and carefully writing out "Sweet. Good cook. Ready for children."

She blew out a breath and wondered if she was the only one stifling in this sudden heat. Ready for children? Hardly. Still...if she was going to make babies with anyone...

Shaking her head to dispel that dangerous image, she found herself at the airport's single baggage carousel. It was just shuddering to life and within moments she pointed out first one, then another sleek, black suitcase. Ethan took them both, began to move toward the door and then faltered to a stop. He avoided her gaze, focusing on something far beyond her shoulder. "It's just...I wasn't...."

Oh God, Autumn thought, a sudden chill racing down her spine. Her stomach lurched and she raised a hand as if to ward off his words. She hadn't even considered this.

He'd taken one look and decided to send her back.

ETHAN STARED INTO THE STRICKEN EYES of the most beautiful woman he'd ever met. He had to confess to her right now the extent of the joke she'd been led into thinking was real. It'd been bad enough when he thought Rob and the rest of them had simply hauled him to the airport for a chance to laugh their asses off at him, but now there was a woman involved, a real, beautiful, fragile woman. He had to stop this before it went any further.

When she raised her clear blue gaze to his, he saw panic, horror, and an awful recognition he instantly realized meant she thought she'd been judged and found wanting. He knew he'd do anything to make that look go away. Judged wanting. As if. The girl was as beautiful as a harvest moon shining on frost-flecked fields in late November. He itched to touch her, take her hand, pull her hard against him and...

Whoa—that thought couldn't go any farther.

He swallowed hard and tried again. "I...it's just my place...something came up and I didn't get a chance to fix it like I meant to." She relaxed a fraction and he rushed on. "It's a good house—built by my great granddaddy in 1889 for the hired help. Solid. Just needs a little attention."

"A woman's touch," Rob threw in.

Ethan restrained himself, barely. He'd get back at all of his friends soon enough. "I just hope you'll be comfortable."

A snigger behind him made him clench his fists.

"I don't mind if it's rough," Autumn said, eliciting a

bark of laughter from the peanut gallery. She blushed and Ethan couldn't take his eyes off her face, although he wished she hadn't caught the joke. She'd look like that in bed, after...

Enough.

"Give me the keys," he said to Rob. When his friend hesitated, he held out a hand. "Now."

Rob handed them over with a raised eyebrow, but Ethan just led the way outside and threw Autumn's suitcases in the bed of the truck. He opened the passenger side door.

"Thank you," she said, putting first one foot, then the other on the running board and scrambling somewhat ungracefully into the seat. City girl. At least her hesitation gave him a long moment to enjoy the view.

Rob made as if to open the door to the back bench seat, but Ethan shoved him aside, pressed down the lock and closed the passenger door. He was halfway around the truck before Rob could react.

"Hey, what are you doing?"

"Taking a ride with my fiancee. You all find your own way home." He was in the driver's side with the ignition turning over before any of them moved a muscle. Stupid fools. They'd made their beds and they could sleep in them.

He glanced at the ethereal princess sitting less than two feet away. Meanwhile, he'd sleep in his own comfortable bed tonight. Maybe with a little company for once.

The **Cowboys of Chance Creek** series continues with
The Cowboy's E-Mail Order Bride.

Be the first to know about Cora Seton's new releases!
Sign up for her newsletter here!
www.coraseton.com/sign-up-for-my-newsletter

Other books in the Cowboys of Chance Creek Series:

The Cowboy's E-mail Order Bride (Volume 1)
The Cowboy Wins a Bride (Volume 2)
The Cowboy Imports a Bride (Volume 3)
The Cowgirl Ropes a Billionaire (Volume 4)
The Sheriff Catches a Bride (Volume 5)
The Cowboy Lassos a Bride (Volume 6)
The Cowboy Rescues a Bride (Volume 7)
The Cowboy Earns a Bride (Volume 8)

Look for the **Heroes of Chance Creek** series, too:

The Navy SEAL's E-mail Order Bride (Volume 1)
The Soldier's E-Mail Order Bride (Volume 2)
The Marine's E-Mail Order Bride (Volume 3)
The Navy SEAL's Christmas Bride (Volume 4)
The Airman's E-Mail Order Bride (Volume 5)

Sign up for my newsletter HERE.
www.coraseton.com/sign-up-for-my-newsletter

Check out Cora Seton's other series, **Heroes of Chance Creek**, which begins with **The Navy SEAL's E-Mail Order Bride**. Read on for an excerpt.

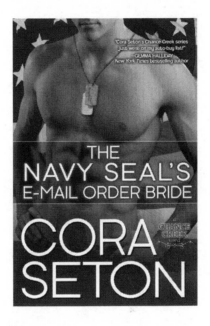

"Boys," Lieutenant Commander Mason Hall said, "we're going home."

He sat back in his folding chair and waited for a reaction from his brothers. The recreation hall at Bagram Airfield was as busy as always with men hunched over laptops, watching the widescreen television, or lounging in groups of three or four shooting the breeze. His brothers—three tall, broad shouldered men in uniform—stared back at him from his computer screen, the feeds from their four-way video conversation all relaying a similar reaction to his words.

Utter confusion.

"Home?" Austin was the first to speak. A Special Forces officer just a year younger than Mason, he was currently in Kabul.

"Home," Mason confirmed. "I got a letter from Great Aunt Heloise. Uncle Zeke passed away over the weekend without designating an heir. That means the ranch reverts back to her. She thinks we'll do a better job running it than Darren will." Darren, their first cousin, wasn't known for his responsible behavior and he hated ranching. Mason, on the other hand, loved it. He had missed the ranch, the cattle, the Montana sky and his family's home ever since they'd left it twelve years ago.

"She's giving Crescent Hall to us?" That was Zane, Austin's twin, a Marine currently in Kandahar. The excitement in his tone told Mason all he needed to know—Zane stilled loved the old place as much as he did. When Mason had gotten Heloise's letter, he'd had to read it more than once before he believed it. The Hall would belong to them once more—when he'd thought they'd lost it for good. Suddenly he'd felt like he could breathe fully again after so many years of holding in his anger and frustration over his uncle's behavior. The timing was perfect, too. He was due to ship stateside any day now. By April he'd be a civilian again.

Except it wasn't as easy as all that. Mason took a deep breath. "There are a few conditions."

Colt, his youngest brother, snorted. "Of course— we're talking about Heloise, aren't we? What's she up to this time?" He was an Air Force combat controller who had served both in Afghanistan and as part of the relief effort a few years back after the massive earthquake which devastated Haiti. He was currently back on United States soil in Florida, training with his unit.

Mason knew what he meant. Calling Heloise eccentric would be an understatement. In her eighties, she had definite opinions and brooked no opposition to her plans and schemes. She meant well, but as his father had always said, she was capable of leaving a swath of destruction in family affairs that rivaled Sherman's march to Atlanta.

"The first condition is that we have to stock the ranch with one hundred pair of cattle within twelve months of taking possession."

"We should be able to do that," Austin said.

"It's going to take some doing to get that ranch up and running again," Zane countered. "Zeke was already letting the place go years ago."

"You have something better to do than fix the place up when you get out?" Mason asked him. He hoped Zane understood the real question: was he in or out?

"I'm in; I'm just saying," Zane said.

Mason suppressed a smile. Zane always knew what he was thinking.

"Good luck with all that," Colt said.

"Thanks," Mason told him. He'd anticipated that inheriting the Hall wouldn't change Colt's mind about staying in the Air Force. He focused on the other two who were both already in the process of winding down their military careers. "If we're going to do this, it'll take a commitment. We're going to have to pool our funds and put our shoulders to the wheel for as long as it takes. Are you up for that?"

"I'll join you there as soon as I'm able to in June," Austin said. "It'll just be like another year in the service. I can handle that."

"I already said I'm in," Zane said. "I'll have boots on the ground in September."

Here's where it got tricky. "There's just one other thing," Mason said. "Aunt Heloise has one more requirement of each of us."

"What's that?" Austin asked when he didn't go on.

"She's worried about the lack of heirs on our side of the family. Darren has children. We don't."

"Plenty of time for that," Zane said. "We're still young, right?"

"Not according to Heloise." Mason decided to get it over and done with. "She's decided that in order for us to inherit the Hall free and clear, we each have to be married within the year. One of us has to have a child."

Stunned silence met this announcement until Colt started to laugh. "Staying in the Air Force doesn't look so bad now, does it?"

"That means you, too," Mason said.

"What? Hold up, now." Colt was startled into soberness. "I won't even live on the ranch. Why do I have to get hitched?"

"Because Heloise says it's time to stop screwing around. And she controls the land. And you know

Heloise."

"How are we going to get around that?" Austin asked.

"We're not." Mason got right to the point. "We're going to find ourselves some women and we're going to marry them."

"In Afghanistan?" Zane's tone made it clear what he thought about that idea.

Tension tightened Mason's jaw. He'd known this was going to be a messy conversation. "Online. I created an online personal ad for all of us. Each of us has a photo, a description and a reply address. A woman can get in touch with whichever of us she chooses and start a conversation. Just weed through your replies until you find the one you want."

"Are you out of your mind?" Zane peered at him through the video screen.

"I don't see what you're upset about. I'm the one who has to have a child. None of you will be out of the service in time."

"Wait a minute—I thought you just got the letter from Heloise." As usual, Austin zeroed in on the inconsistency.

"The letter came about a week ago. I didn't want to get anyone's hopes up until I checked a few things out." Mason shifted in his seat. "Heloise said the place is in rougher shape than we thought. Sounds like Zeke sold off the last of his cattle last year. We're going to have to start from scratch, and we're going to have to move fast to meet her deadline—on both counts. I did all the leg work on the online ad. All you need to do is read some e-mails, look at some photos and pick one. How hard can that be?"

"I'm beginning to think there's a reason you've been single all these years, Straightshot," Austin said. Mason winced at the use of his nickname. The men in his unit had christened him with it during his early days in the service, but as Colt said when his brothers had first heard about it, it made perfect sense. The name had little to do with his accuracy with a rifle, and everything to do with his tendency to find the shortest route from here to done on any mission he was tasked with. Regardless of what obstacles stood in his way.

Colt snickered. "Told you two it was safer to stay in the military. Mason's Matchmaking Service. It has a ring to it. I guess you've found yourself a new career, Mase."

"Stow it." Mason tapped a finger on the table. "Just because I've put the ad up doesn't mean that any of you have to make contact with the women who write you. If it doesn't work, it doesn't work. But you need to marry within the year. If you don't find a wife for yourself, I'll find one for you."

"He would, too," Austin said to the others. "You know he would."

"When does the ad go live?" Zane asked.

"It went live five days ago. You've each got several hundred responses so far. I'll forward them to you as soon as we break the call."

Austin must have leaned toward his webcam because suddenly he filled the screen. "Several hundred?"

"That's right."

Colt's laughter rang out over the line.

"Don't know what you're finding so funny, Colton," Mason said in his best imitation of their late father's voice. "You've got several hundred responses, too."

"What? I told you I was staying…"

"Read through them and answer all the likely ones. I'll be in touch in a few days to check your progress." Mason cut the call.

* * *

Regan Anderson wanted a baby. Right now. Not five years from now. Not even next year.

Right now.

And since she'd just quit her stuffy loan officer job, moved out of her overpriced one bedroom New York City apartment, and completed all her preliminary appointments, she was going to get one via the modern technology of artificial insemination.

As she raced up the three flights of steps to her tiny new studio, she took the pins out of her severe updo and let her thick, auburn hair swirl around her shoulders. By the time she reached the door, she was breathing hard. Inside, she shut and locked it behind her, tossed her briefcase and blazer on the bed which took up the lion's share of the living space, and kicked off her high heels. Her blouse and pencil skirt came next, and thirty seconds later she was down to her skivvies.

Thank God.

She was done with Town and Country Bank. Done with originating loans for people who would scrape and slave away for the next thirty years just to cling to a lousy flat near a subway stop. She was done, done, done being a cog in the wheel of a financial system she couldn't stand to be a part of anymore.

She was starting a new business. Starting a new life.

And she was starting a family, too.

Alone.

After years of looking for Mr. Right, she'd decided he simply didn't exist in New York City. So after several medical exams and consultations, she had scheduled her first round of artificial insemination for the end of April. She couldn't wait.

Meanwhile, she'd throw herself into the task of building her consulting business. She would make it her job to help non-profits assist regular people start new stores and services, buy homes that made sense, and manage their money so that they could get ahead. It might not be as lucrative as being a loan officer, but at least she'd be able to sleep at night.

She wasn't going to think about any of that right now, though. She'd survived her last day at work, survived her exit interview, survived her boss, Jack Richey, pretending to care that she was leaving. Now she was giving herself the weekend off. No work, no nothing—just forty-eight hours of rest and relaxation.

Having grabbed takeout from her favorite Thai restaurant on the way home, Regan spooned it out onto a plate and carried it to her bed. Lined with pillows, it doubled as her couch during waking hours. She sat cross-legged on top of the duvet and savored her food and her freedom. She had bought herself a nice bottle of wine to drink this weekend, figuring it might be her last for an awfully long time. She was all too aware her Chardonnay-sipping days were coming to an end. As soon as her weekend break from reality was over, she planned to spend the next ten months starting her business, while scrimping and saving every penny she could. She would have to move to a bigger apartment right before the baby was born, but given the cost of renting in the city, the temporary downgrade was worth it. She pushed all thoughts of business and the future out of her mind. Rest and relax—that was her job for now.

Two hours and two glasses of wine later, however, rest and relaxation was beginning to feel a lot like loneliness and boredom. In truth, she'd been fighting loneliness for months. She'd broken up with her last boyfriend before Christmas. Here it was March and she was still single. Two of her closest friends had gotten married and moved away in the past twelve months, Laurel to New Hampshire and Rita to New Jersey. They rarely saw each other now and when she'd jokingly mentioned the idea of going ahead and having a child without a husband the last time they'd gotten together, both women had scoffed.

"No way could I have gotten through this pregnancy without Ryan." Laurel ran a hand over her large belly. "I've felt awful the whole time."

"No way I'm going back to work." Rita's baby was six weeks old. "Thank God Alan brings in enough cash to see us through."

Regan decided not to tell them about her plans until the pregnancy was a done deal. She knew what she was getting into—she didn't need them to tell her how hard it might be. If there'd been any way for her to have a baby normally—with a man she loved—she'd have chosen that path in a heartbeat. But there didn't seem to be a man for her to love in New York. Unfortunately, keeping her secret meant it was hard to call either Rita or Laurel just to chat, and she needed someone to chat with tonight. As dusk descended on the city, Regan felt fear for the first time since making her decision to go ahead with having a child.

What if she'd made a mistake? What if her consultancy business failed? What if she became a welfare mother? What if she had to move back home?

When the thoughts and worries circling her mind grew overwhelming, she topped up her wine, opened up her laptop and clicked on a YouTube video of a cat stuck headfirst in a cereal box. Thank goodness she'd hooked up wi-fi the minute she secured the studio. Simultaneously scanning her Facebook feed, she read an update from an acquaintance named Susan who was exhibiting her art in one of the local galleries. She'd have to stop by this weekend.

She watched a couple more videos—the latest installment in a travel series she loved, and one about over-the-top weddings that made her sad. Determined to cheer up, she hopped onto Pinterest and added more images to her nursery pinboard. Sipping her wine, she checked the news, posted a question on the single parents' forum she frequented, checked her e-mail again, and then tapped a finger on the keys, wondering what to do next. The evening stretched out before her, vacant even of the work she normally took home to do over the weekend. She hadn't felt at such loose ends in years.

Pacing her tiny apartment didn't help. Nor did an attempt at unpacking more of her things. She had finished moving in just last night and boxes still lined one wall. She opened one to reveal books, took a look at her limited shelf space and packed them up again. A second box revealed her collection of vintage fans. No room for them here, either.

She stuck her iTouch into a docking station and turned up some tunes, then drained her glass, poured herself another, and flopped onto her bed. The wine was beginning to take effect—giving her a nice, soft, fuzzy feeling. It hadn't done away with her loneliness, but when she turned back to Facebook on her laptop, the images and YouTube links seemed funnier this time.

Heartened, she scrolled further down her feed until she spotted another post one of her friends had shared. It was an image of a handsome man standing ramrod straight in combat fatigues. *Hello.* He was cute. In fact, he looked like exactly the kind of man she'd always hoped she'd meet. He wasn't thin and arrogant like the up-and-coming Wall Street crowd, or paunchy and cynical like the upper-management men who hung around the bars near work. Instead he looked healthy, muscle-bound, clear-sighted, and vital. What was the post about? She clicked the link underneath it. Maybe there'd be more fantasy-fodder like this man wherever it took her.

There *was* more fantasy fodder. Regan wriggled happily. She had landed on a page that showcased four men. Brothers, she saw, looking more closely—two of them identical twins. Each one seemed to represent a different branch of the United States military. Were they models? Was this some kind of recruitment ploy?

Practical Wives Wanted read the heading at the top. Regan nearly spit out a sip of her wine. Wives Wanted? Practical ones? She considered the men again, then read more.

Looking for a change? the text went on. *Ready for a real challenge? Join four hardworking, clean living men and help bring our family's ranch back to life.*

Skills required—any or all of the following: Riding, roping, construction, animal care, roofing, farming, market gardening, cooking, cleaning, metalworking, small motor repair…

The list went on and on. Regan bit back at a laugh which quickly dissolved into giggles. Small engine repair? How very romantic. Was this supposed to be satire or was it real? It was certainly one of the most intriguing things she'd seen online in a long, long time.

Must be willing to commit to a man and the project. No weekends/no holidays/no sick days. Weaklings need not apply.

Regan snorted. It was beginning to sound like an

employment ad. Good luck finding a woman to fill those conditions. She'd tried to find a suitable man for years and came up with Erik—the perennial mooch who'd finally admitted just before Christmas that he liked her old Village apartment more than he liked her. That's why she planned to get pregnant all by herself. There wasn't anyone worth marrying in the whole city. Probably the whole state. And if the men were all worthless, the women probably were, too. She reached for her wine without turning from the screen, missed, and nearly knocked over her glass. She tried again, secured the wine, drained the glass a third time and set it down again.

What she would give to find a real partner. Someone strong, both physically and emotionally. An equal in intelligence and heart. A real man.

But those didn't exist.

If you're sick of wasting your time in a dead-end job, tired of tearing things down instead of building something up, or just ready to get your hands dirty with clean, honest work, write and tell us why you'd make a worthy wife for a man who has spent the last decade in uniform.

There wasn't much to laugh at in this paragraph. Regan read it again, then got up and wandered to the kitchen to top up her glass. She'd never seen a singles ad like this one. She could see why it was going viral. If it was real, these men were something special. Who wanted to do clean, honest work these days? What kind of man was selfless enough to serve in the military instead of sponging off their girlfriends? If she'd known there were guys like this in the world, she might not have been so quick to schedule the artificial insemination appointment.

She wouldn't cancel it, though, because these guys couldn't be for real, and she wasn't waiting another minute to start her family. She had dreamed of having children ever since she was a child herself and organized pretend schools in her backyard for the neighborhood little ones. Babies loved her. Toddlers thought she was the next best thing to teddy bears. Her co-workers at the bank had never appreciated her as much as the average five-year-old did.

Further down the page there were photographs of the ranch the brothers meant to bring back to life. The land was beautiful, if overgrown, but its toppled fences and sagging buildings were a testament to its neglect. The photograph of the main house caught her eye and kept her riveted, though. A large gothic structure, it could be beautiful with the proper care. She could see why these men would dedicate themselves to returning it to its former glory. She tried to imagine what it would be like to live on the ranch with one of them, and immediately her body craved an open sunny sky—the kind you were hard pressed to see in the city. She sunk into the daydream, picturing herself sitting on a back porch sipping lemonade while her cowboy worked and the baby napped. Her husband would have his shirt off while he chopped wood, or mended a fence or whatever it was ranchers did. At the end of the day they'd fall into bed and make love until morning.

Regan sighed. It was a wonderful daydream, but it had no bearing on her life. Disgruntled, she switched over to Netflix and set up a foreign film. She fetched the bottle of wine back to bed with her and leaned against her many pillows. She'd managed to hang her small flatscreen on the opposite wall. In an apartment this tiny, every piece of furniture needed to serve double-duty.

As the movie started, Regan found herself composing messages to the military men in the Wife Wanted ad, in which she described herself as trim and petite, or lithe and strong, or horny and good-enough-looking to do the trick.

An hour later, when the film failed to hold her attention, she grabbed her laptop again. She pulled up the Wife Wanted page and reread it, keeping an eye on the foreign couple on the television screen who alternately argued and kissed.

Crazy what some people did. What was wrong with these men that they needed to advertise for wives instead of going out and meeting them like normal people?

She thought of the online dating sites she'd tried in the past. She'd had some awkward experiences, some horrible first dates, and finally one relationship that lasted for a couple of months before the man was transferred to Tucson and it fizzled out. It hadn't worked for her, but she supposed lots of people found love online these days. They might not advertise directly for spouses, but that was their ultimate intention, right?

So maybe this ad wasn't all that unusual.

Most men who posted singles ads weren't as hot as these men were, though. Definitely not the ones she'd met. She poured herself another glass. A small twinge of her conscience told her she'd already had far too much wine for a single night.

To hell with that, Regan thought. As soon as she got pregnant she'd have to stay sober and sane for the next eighteen years. She wouldn't have a husband to trade off with—she'd always be the designated driver, the adult in charge, the sober, wise mother who made sure nothing bad ever happened to her child. Just this one last time she was allowed to blow off steam.

But even as she thought it, a twinge of fear wormed through her belly.

What if she wasn't good enough?

She stood up, strode the two steps to the kitchenette and made herself a bowl of popcorn. She drowned it in butter and salt, returned to the bed in time for the ending credits of the movie, and lined up *Pride and Prejudice* with Colin Firth. Time for comfort food and a comfort movie. *Pride and Prejudice* always did the trick when she felt blue. She checked the Wife Wanted page again on her laptop. If she was going to pick one of the men—which she wasn't—who would she choose?

Mason, the oldest, due to leave the Navy in a matter of weeks, drew her eye first. With his dark crew cut, hard jaw and uncompromising blue eyes he looked like the epitome of a military man. He stated his interests as ranching—of course—history, natural sciences and tactical operations, whatever the hell that was. That left her little more informed than before she'd read it, and she wondered what the man was really like. Did he read the newspaper in bed on Sunday mornings? Did he prefer lasagna or spaghetti? Would he listen to country music in his truck or talk radio? She stared at his photo, willing him to answer.

The next two brothers, Austin and Zane, were less fierce, but looked no less intelligent and determined. Still, they didn't draw her eye the way the way Mason did. Colt, the youngest, was blond with a grin she bet drew women like flies. That one was trouble, and she didn't need trouble.

She read Mason's description again and decided he was the leader of this endeavor. If she was going to pick one, it would be him.

But she wasn't going to pick one. She had given up all that. She'd made a promise to her imaginary child that she would not allow any chaos into its life. No dating until her baby wore a graduation gown, at the very least. She felt another twinge. Was she ready to give up men for nearly two decades? That was a long time.

It's worth it, she told herself. She had no doubt about her desire to be a mother. She had no doubt she'd be a great mom. She was smart, capable and had a good head on her shoulders. She was funny, silly and patient, too. She loved children.

She was just lousy with men.

But that didn't matter anymore. She pushed the laptop aside and returned her attention to *Pride and Prejudice*, quickly falling into an old drinking game she and Laurel had devised one night that required taking a swig of wine each time one of the actresses lifted her eyebrows in polite surprise. When she finished the bottle, she headed to the tiny kitchenette to track down another one, trilling, "Jane! Elizabeth!" at the top of her voice along with Mrs. Bennett in the film. There was no more wine, so she switched to tequila.

By the time Elizabeth Bennett discovered the miracle of Mr. Darcy's palace-sized mansion, and decided she'd been too hasty in turning down his offer of marriage, Regan had decided she too needed to cast off her prejudices and find herself a man. A hot hunk of a military man. She grabbed the laptop, fumbled with the link that would let her leave Mason Hall a message and drafted a brilliant missive worthy of Jane Austen herself.

Dear Lt. Cmdr. Hall,

In her mind she pronounced lieutenant with an "f" like the Brits in the movie onscreen.

It is a truth universally acknowledged, that a single man in possession of a good ranch, must be in want of a wife. Furthermore, it must be self-evident that the wife in question should possess certain qualities numbering amongst them riding, roping, construction, roofing, farming, market gardening, cooking, cleaning, metalworking, animal care, and—most importantly, by Heaven—small motor repair.

    Seeing as I am in possession of all these qualities, not to mention many others you can only have left out through unavoidable oversight or sheer obtuseness—such as glassblowing, cheesemaking, towel origami, heraldry, hovercraft piloting, and an uncanny sense of what cats are thinking—I feel almost forced to catapult myself into your purview.

You will see from my photograph that I am most eminently and majestically suitable for your wife.

She inserted a digital photo of her foot.

In fact, one might wonder why such a paragon of virtue such as I should deign to answer such a peculiar advertisement. The truth is, sir, that I long for adventure. To get my hands dirty with clean, hard work. To build something up instead of tearing it down.

In short, you are really hot. I'd like to lick you.

Yours,
Regan Anderson

On screen, Elizabeth Bennett lifted an eyebrow. Regan knocked back another shot of Jose Cuervo and passed out.

End of Excerpt

The Navy SEAL's E-mail Order Bride (Volume 1)

Other books in the **Heroes of Chance Creek** series:

The Soldier's E-Mail Order Bride (Volume 2)
The Marine's E-Mail Bride (Volume 3)
The Navy SEAL's Christmas Bride (Volume 4)
The Airman's E-Mail Order Bride (Volume 5)

About the Author

Cora Seton loves cowboys, country life, gardening, bike-riding, and lazing around with a good book. Mother of four, wife to a computer programmer/ eco-farmer, she ditched her California lifestyle nine years ago and moved to a remote logging town in northwestern British Columbia. Like the characters in her novels, Cora enjoys old-fashioned pursuits and modern technology, spending mornings transforming an ordinary one-acre lot into a paradise of orchards, berry bushes and market gardens, and afternoons writing the latest Chance Creek romance novel on her iPad mini. Visit www.coraseton.com to read about new releases and learn about contests and other events!

Blog:
http://www.coraseton.com

Facebook:
http://www.facebook.com/coraseton

Twitter:
http://www.twitter.com/coraseton

Made in the USA
Charleston, SC
03 October 2015